# Playing the Game

A Core Four Series Novella

M. George

ISBN:
978-1-969305-99-3 (PAPERBACK)
978-1-969305-00-9 (HARDBACK)
978-1-969305-01-6 (DISCREET PAPERBACK)
978-1-969305-02-3 (DISCREET HARDBACK)
978-1-969305-98-6 (EBOOK)

LIBRARY OF CONGRESS CONTROL NUMBER: 2025917133

COVER DESIGN: M. GEORGE
IMAGES: CANVA PRO/SHUTTERSTOCK PHOTOS
FORMATTING: AFFINITY PUBLISHER/VELLUM
FIRST EDITION: SEPTEMBER 2025

FOR MAYA. FOR
JEFF. I WILL
ALWAYS LOVE YOU,
AND I WILL ALWAYS
MISS YOU.

# DEDICATION

FOR ALL THE GOOD GIRLS WHO DREAM OF GETTING RAILED IN A SEX CLUB BY A MYSTERIOUS STRANGER. LIFE'S TOO SHORT, BABE. GO CROSS THEM OFF YOUR BUCKET LIST.

M. George

# IMPORTANT NOTE

THIS BOOK CONTAINS CONTENT THAT IS NOT SUITABLE FOR ALL READERS. BEFORE PROCEEDING, PLEASE BE MINDFUL OF THE FACT THAT THIS BOOK CONTAINS DARK THEMES AND SCENES CONTAINING THE FOLLOWING:

-DRUG USE

-USE OF DATE RAPE DRUGS

-MENTIONS OF GRIEF/DEATH OF A PARTNER

-OBSESSIVE/POSSESSIVE MMC

-STALKING

-LIGHT BDSM PLAY (DOM/SUB LIGHT)

-MENTIONS OF VOYEURISM

-MENTIONS OF BONDAGE/LIGHT ROPE PLAY

-MENTIONS OF BREATH PLAY

-MENTIONS OF PAST TRAUMA/ABUSE

-NIGHTMARES

-PTSD/ANXIET Y

-MENTIONS OF TEEN PREGNANCY/PARENTHOOD

THIS CONTENT IS ALSO AVAILABLE ON MY SOCIAL MEDIA PAGES AND MY WEBSITE AT WWW.MGEORGEAUTHOR.COM

PLEASE TAKE NOTE OF THE ABOVE LISTED CONTENT AND BE MINDFUL OF ANY PERSONAL TRIGGERS THAT YOU MAY HAVE. YOUR MENTAL HEALTH MATTERS.

THANK YOU.

# OFFICIAL PLAYLIST

BUCKET LIST (PIANO VERSION) - MITCHELL TENPENNY

GIRL ALL THE BAD GUYS WANT - BOWLING FOR SOUP

"IF THESE SCARS COULD SPEAK" - CITIZEN SOLDIER

SCARS - PAPA ROACH

CONFIDENT - DEMI LOVATO

HANDCLAP - FITZ AND THE TANTRUMS

POWERFUL - MAJOR LAZER & ELLIE GOULDING (FT. TARRUS RILEY)

DANGEROUS - SLEEP TOKEN

SATISFY - NERO

APHRODITE - SAM SHORT

MEDUSA - AMANATI

TREACHEROUS - TAYLOR SWIFT (TAYLOR'S VERSION)

COWBOW LIKE ME - TAYLOR SWIFT

FOR THE GIRLS - ASTON

INTO THE NIGHT - NERO

TAKE ME TO CHURCH - HOZIER

CALL YOU MINE - THE CHAINSMOKERS (FT. BEBE REXHA)

# Eli and Quincy's Bucket List

1. Travel the world together

2. ~~Own who you are~~

3. See Glitterpus and Jericho live in concert

4. Experience the Northern Lights in person

5. Go Skydiving ~~and Ziplining~~

6. ~~Get a tattoo. Get many tattoos~~

7. ~~Learn a new language~~

8. Become an audiobook narrator

9. Visit Germany for Oktoberfest

10. Travel through Scotland

11. Learn to ballroom dance

12. Try every single menu item from one restaurant

13. ~~Start a business~~

14. Embrace something kinky that would horrify our parents

15. Learn to ice skate

16. Tour the catacombs in Paris and other haunted places around Europe.

17. Get locked in a library over night

18. Drive a construction vehicle - backhoe or excavator

19. Visit a sex club

20. Marry my best friend

21. ~~Become a mom~~

22. ~~Escape the conservative hell hole I call home~~

23. Finish the list for Eli

# Chapter One

## Quincy

Sissy: You look HOTT!!!

Goldie: Fuck that, you are smokin'!

Should I be doing this???

Goldie: You remember what Dr. Sandsworth said, QT. Besides, you are a total BABE. A literal motherduckin' MILF.

Goldie: Motherducking

Goldie: Motherforker!

Goldie: Ahhhh!

Goldie: Damn autocorrect!

Goldie: *Motherfucking

Sissy: So help me, if you waste this opportunity I will jump through the phone and . . .

Sissy: . . .

And what?

Sissy: I don't know. I was trying to come up with something impressive enough to push you into going.

Sissy: Oh! I know! I will jump through the phone and have Danni kick your ass.

Goldie: *Laugh emoji*

Sissy: We both know she could.

Not gonna happen. Goldie here loves me, I'm her favorite, remember? Since I gave her such a cute godson and all. . .

Goldie: True, true.

Goldie: Besides, with the work you have done with Jay, I'm sure you could just as easily pin my ass to the ground.

Sissy: . . .

Goldie: . . .

You know I love you, but not like that. Right?

Like, girl you are HOTT but I think Daddy Theo would tan my hide if I turned your twosome into a threesome and made him a Daddy for real. . .

Goldie: . . . yeah, yeah. I saw it after I sent it *insert eye roll*

Not that I would mind him giving me a good spanking *devil grin-face emoji* *pepper emoji*

Goldie: I'm gonna choose not to respond to that last comment.

Sissy: OH GOOD! Cuz, I was totally gonna say it but Con says I need to work on my filter a bit.

You're still seeing that asshole?

Sissy: Hey! Connor is great! He just. . . has a lot on his plate and gets overwhelmed sometimes. You know how it is. *shrugs*

No, explain it to me. 'Cuz last time I checked, you went through the SAME med school program as he did, put in the same work and effort, and managed to do so without being a complete jackass.

Goldie: *snorts*

Goldie: At least most of the time.

Sissy: Hey! Whose side are you on, anyway?

Goldie: Well. . . your sister did birth this really freaking cute kid and let me be his godmother and all, so . . .

Sissy: . . .

Sissy: Well. . . I see how the turn-tables turn. . .

You know that's not the phrase, right?

Sissy: OBVIOUSLY

Sissy: Don't judge me.

You are inspiring such faith in your doctoring abilities right now.

Sissy: Hey!

The medical field should be shaking in their boots right now.

Sissy: RUDE

Sissy: I take offense to that!

Sissy: If nothing else, I am a kick-ass doctor, thank you very much!

Ok, can we please circle back to my original question?

Sissy: I forgot, what was it again?

Goldie: Yeah, me too. What were we talking about?

You GUYS. You can literally just scroll through our texts *eye roll*

Should I be doing this?

Sissy: Aside from the fact that this was something you discussed with Dr. Sandsworth, as Danni already said. . .

Sissy: This is on your bucket list. I think you need to do this.

Goldie: Eli would want you to do this. He would think you are a sexy badass for doing this on your own too.

Sissy: Besides, do you know the kind of connections I had to pull to get you access to this club? This isn't your average, run-of-the-mill sex club.

Sissy: This club is exclusive.

Sissy: Millionaires go there. Singers. Actors.

Sissy: Athletes...

Sissy: Who knows, maybe you will find yourself a rich, sexy-as-hell man to fuck all those cares right out of your head?

Goldie: Or woman!

Or woman!

Sissy: Again, obviously. That point goes without being said.

Or not, since we both said it.

Sissy: Well I thought the relationship with your last girlfriend kinda stated the obvious there. Apparently not.

Goldie: Say hi to Simone for me when you see her btw.

Goldie: Oh, and Layonna!

Sissy: What she said!

Sissy: But also. . . maybe you will find yourself a rich, sexy-as-hell person to fuck all those cares right out of your head

Sissy: Oh! Or even fall in love with you!

Better. Thank you.

Goldie: Find her soulmate at a sex-club? Now that would be a fucking dream come true.

Goldie: Ha! See what I did there? *Waggles eyebrows suggestively*

Yes, yes. I'm so sure you guys.

I'm gonna find me a rich, hot-as-sin fuck-god(ess) who is gonna sex me into oblivion and whisk me away on a magical flying carpet made from thousand dollar bills to be the Prince/ess Charming to my Cinderella. Is that it?

Goldie: Yep

Sissy: Sounds about right.

Uh-huh. You guys are no help at all.

Sissy: STFU, stop texting us and go get laid bitch!

Ah, just what every girl wants to hear from her older sister.

Shoving the phone in my clutch, I smooth down my very see-through black lace top. The theme is Candy Cane Masquerade. All women are encouraged to dress in candy cane colors - red or white - and have some sort of mask. I couldn't find anything matching the theme that would fit though. The best I could come up with is a red ribbon to keep my hair out of my face and matching boots, to add a pop of holiday color against my black lace corset. I'm not sure what the dress code is for the men. Pretty sure I recall reading something about them being required to wear all black for the event, so hopefully I won't stand out like a sore thumb. Although, I suppose that is the whole point of my going tonight.

Who knows if I'm even going to hook up with anyone, though. The terms of the bucket list were ambiguous. Originally when Eli added that little note on the list, the insinuation was that we would go explore and play together. Some of the items had been intended for either of us to do solo. This one, however, had been the result of a delirious late night conversation and joking around about what sort of things would make the throbbing vein in his zealous preacher father's head combust, to say nothing of my own parents. I never would've imagined that four years later I would be doing this on my own. . .

Calgary
Cougars

# Chapter Two

## *Bash*

The roar of the crowd pulses through my veins as the crisp air cools my overheated skin. Pumping my fist in excitement as the siren sounds the final goal, I make quick work of skating over to my teammates, slapping each of them on the back as we cluster together in a fucking celebration sandwich. At 4-0,  we ended this game with a fucking shutout, and I just scored the winning goal, thank you very much.

I can't help the shit-eating grin that crosses my face as my teammates continue congratulating me while the crowd cheers us on.Looking up into the stands, I throw a wink to a group of fans pushing against the plexiglass and hear some chick shriek my name like a banshee. Chuckling, I shake my head as I do a quick victory lap, waving good-naturedly to the fans which elicits even more cheers from the stands as I make my way off the ice to hit the locker room.

"Yo Tricky,"

Toweling off my damp hair, I glance over to Johanes who is now standing by the exit.

"You coming or what, man?"

Most of the guys from the team have already left, off to hit up the latest club to celebrate our W. He eyes me expectantly, but I just shake my head.

"Nah man, I'm good. You go ahead."

Johanes groans, frustration evident. "Dude! What is with you lately? Come on, man. You used to be the life of the party, but you've bailed after like the last five games. What the hell?"

He's right, of course. Normally, I am the life of the party, the pusher, the one who keeps the party going all night long. I don't know what the hell is wrong with me, other than I am just tired. I'm tired of the same old shit, day in and day out; tired of the same women throwing themselves at us game after game.

Don't get me wrong. I love my boys, and hanging with them

after another W is always chill.But the music, the plastered smiles, the nauseating perfume that these puck bunnies seem to fucking bathe in? I am just so fucking tired of the bullshit. I can't say that, however. Instead, I simply shrug, throwing my signature grin his way.

"Can't man. I've got. . . plans tonight," I throw his way with a wink, the insinuation clear.

He snorts, shaking his head. "Right. I get it. You've got your pick of the puck bunnies lined up and waiting for you already. Hell man, why didn't you just say so? More for the rest of us, I guess." Johanes wags his eyebrows in an exaggerated manner before jerking his chin towards me. "Give her a kiss for me, will ya?" He grins as he slowly backs out the door, "Later dude!"

I swallow my disgust from his response, turning back to grab my shit.

The room is quiet as I sit in the stillness of the dark room, staring blankly at the screen playing a recap of tonight's game, my beer having long since gone warm after sitting forgotten on the table next to me.

"Ugh!" I groan, running a ragged hand through my still-damp hair. After quickly changing, I had nothing better to do than to head home and watch the game footage on replay. But beer and the quiet is just not doing it for me.

"Fucking hell." With a low grumble, I glance down at my watch. I've been sitting here for almost an hour since getting home, but for the life of me I haven't been able to focus. Shit.

The guys will be just hitting their stride at the club right about now, drinks and beautiful women swarming them in the VIP section. I could go hang out for an hour or two, tell them that my plans have changed. . . but damn. I just don't have it in me to plaster on that fake as fuck smile all the ladies love, the ones my teammates have come to expect from me.

But sitting here zoning out in front of the television isn't doing it for me either. Fuck this shit. Reaching for the remote, I shut off the game, stretching out my aching joints as I stand. Maybe a good night's rest is what I need to get me out of this funk.

Making my way through the spacious apartment, I head straight for the master suite. I don't bother turning on the lights as I make my way into the bedroom. Out of habit, I toss my phone and wallet onto the nightstand, kicking off my shorts and throwing back the covers. Settling onto the cool sheets, I close my eyes. Yep, a good night's rest is all I need.

"Baby, you said you were coming. Why aren't you here yet?" Shouts and drunken laughter make her words difficult to hear. Pressing the phone closer to my ear, I throw an apprehensive glance behind me.

"No, no no no. I can fix this. No, I can fix this. No, no no no. No."

Crouched in a corner, hands fisted in his hair, I watch helplessly as my twin rocks back and forth, muttering to himself as he pulls at the roots. If he keeps this up, he is going to start pulling it out by the fistfull. It's been years since I've seen him this bad, but it's certainly not the first time. Still, I'm worried this will send him spiraling down into another catatonic state, like the one he crashed into after mom left.

"Baby, are you even paying attention to me?"

A shrill voice cuts through my anxious thoughts.

"Sorry, yeah I'm here. Look. I know I promised I'd be there, but I can't tonight. I can't leave Finn alone like this. Not right now."

"You're always blowing me off for him! It's not fair. What about me, Sebastian? When do I come first?"

"Sarah." I sigh, rubbing a hand over my face. "I can't do this right now. Finn needs me. He's my brother. I can't just leave him when he's like this, you know that."

"No, Sebastian. What I know is that I'm always coming second to what you want. It's your brother. Or your hockey. Or your stupid friends. This is important to me. You told me you would come out with me tonight and hang out with my friends for once and now you're blowing me off. Again. I'm sick of it. I'm done being an afterthought to you. I'm a fucking catch, Sebastian. Do you know how many guys I could have slept with over the last two years? How many times I've come to these parties alone while you were doing 'god knows what' with your damn brother and friends and I turned them all down? For you!" Her voice is bordering on hysterical, and I grimace.

"Look, I'm sorry. I know I promised I'd be there but things at home are. . ." I glance behind me at Finn once more, lowering my voice to a whisper. "Well, they're bad right now. I have to take care of this, okay? Just give me some time. A couple of days and then maybe I can take you to a different party next weekend, after things have settled down a bit."

"I'm done playing games Sebastian. It's me, or him. You need to decide. But if you don't get your ass over here like you promised then we are through. Do you hear me? Done!"

"No!" A loud crash behind me sends me jumping, heart racing as I turn to look, dropping my phone.

The room fades into a blur of faces and shouting voices, red and blue lights reflecting bleakly on the icy windowpane. Dread washes over me, trying to drown me but I can't escape this living nightmare. It's all my fault. This is all my fucking fault.

"My baby! No, no no! Not my baby!"

Mrs. Rosenthal collapses against me, her wailing sobs drowning out the somber voices of the two uniformed men standing before us.

Exhaustion weighs me down with their words, guilt settling into my gut with each minute that slowly passes.

"We're so sorry for your loss, Ma'am."

"My baby! They took her from me!" Her voice is near hysterical, and it's all I can do to brace the sobbing woman. "No! No, no no no!" Sinking with her to the floor, my knees hit the cold ground with a painful bite that barely registers through the guilt. Like a gut punch, her distraught cries are a mournful echo of my brother's own downward spiral from just days ago. Back before my whole world was torn apart. And it's all my fault. I did this. She's dead because of me. I –

Shit! Heart racing, I bolt upright, the sheet pooling around my waist as a cold sweat sends chills through me, goosebumps rising on my overheated skin.

Just a dream. It was just a dream.

Groaning, I scrub my face before running my hands through my overgrown hair. Trying to slow my racing heart, I lean over to grab my phone off the nightstand. Tapping the screen, the motion illuminates the clock sitting over the background of my team's logo. Blearily, I glare at the display, as if it were directly to blame for the nightmare that I can't stop reliving, the second hand slowly ticking away as if time itself is mocking me. It's still early, and I've barely been asleep for thirty minutes, but there's no way I'll be able to fall back asleep now. Not after that dream again.

Throwing back the tangled sheets, my feet hit the cool ground and I stumble over to the bathroom. Setting my phone next to me on the counter as I reach for the faucet handle, the cool water does little to erase the painful memories that plague me. The faint blue glow of the motion-sensor lights that line the mirrors softly illuminate my dripping face as I stare bleakly at my reflection.

Hands resting on the counter, all I see is exhaustion lining my face, I almost don't recognize the person staring back at me. Maybe it's time for a change. Maybe the nightmares are my subconscious's way of telling me it's time to do something different with my life.

I don't even know what I want anymore.

Sighing heavily, I reach out to swipe at my phone once more. Unlocking the screen, my fingers travel to the speed dial out of habit. The phone barely rings before I hear a gruff voice on the other end.

"This better be fucking important."

"Nice to talk to you too, dude."

A soft murmur sounds over the line, and I hear the sound of what must be rustling sheets. Shit.

Making my way out of the bathroom, I pass over my bedroom, instead heading to the living room once more, turning on one of the lamps in the corner as I pass by.

"I didn't wake you, did I?" I grimace, regretful as I throw myself down on the couch with a heavy plop.

More murmurs and the distant sound of grumbles that are too hard to make out and then I hear the beep of my FaceTime ringtone. Without hesitation, I swipe to answer.

"Well, hello hotness!" With effort, I paste a grin on my face, forcing a cheerfulness that I don't feel as Danni's face comes into view. An explosion of riotous curls cascade over her shoulders, and her flushed face highlights her ever-present freckles.

"So I didn't wake you, then?" My grin widens, becoming more genuine with the amused realization that I must have interrupted something a bit more. . . vigorous. "How's my favorite girl today?" Danni really is, too; holding a spot that no one else has ever been able to fill. Over the years, she's become one of the most important people to me; the closest thing I will ever have to a sister. She'll always be my favorite girl.

"Trying to celebrate her long-lost boyfriend's win tonight without waking the kid down the hall, thanks for that." Theo's face comes into view now, much grumpier and way less cute than that of his other half.

I have to bite back a laugh as I watch Danica smack Theo in the chest, hard enough to make him wince.

"Be nice. You were the one who answered the phone, anyway." She glares at him before facing the screen once more with a broad smile. "And congrats on your big win tonight, Bash!" Her voice shifts to a low whisper as she glances quickly to Theo before shooting a conspiratorial wink in my direction. "I may or may not have been streaming your game while sitting in the stands watching my man dominate the ice."

I can't help it, a laugh bursts free as Theo gawps at Danni, jaw dropping in shock before he glares at me through the phone. "Are you hearing this right now? I had less than your full attention while I was on the ice?" His voice is indignant as he whispers something in Italian that I don't fucking understand before continuing, "La mia diavoletta, you have been a naughty little devil tonight, hmm?"

"Ew. Dude. I'm right here." Grimacing at their pillow talk, I shake my head in mock disgust. Really, I am happy for them. Ecstatic. One of my best friends is finally getting his happily ever after with the woman who is basically my little sister, after years of drama and a love they both thought they had lost thanks to their asshole family members.

And honestly, it's in no small part thanks to me. If I hadn't pushed Danni to go to that game to watch me play against the Sabretooths, she may never have run into Theo again, and the dominoes may never have fallen into place that inevitably led to their reunion. Just call me Cupid, I guess.

"Hey, you're the one who called us in the middle of the night. Don't be mad at me for having a moment with my woman!" I swear, Danni has hearts coming out of her eyes as Theo calls her 'his woman.' Ladies, am I right?

"C'mon, Giovanni. Lest you forget, you were the one who chose to answer the phone in the first place. How was I to know, sitting here all by my lonesome, that when I called I would be interrupting. . . your celebrations? And honestly, why the fuck did you answer your phone at all? If I had a smokin' woman in my bed as hot as Kitty Cat over there, I sure as hell wouldn't be answering my phone to talk to the likes of me."

Theo coughs, holding back a laugh, but Danni places a hand on his shoulder as she responds. "I made him answer. I knew you wouldn't call this late unless it was important. What's up?" Her eyes are soft, and she gives me that look. The one she always has for me and Finn. My twin and I, along with her brother Caleb, are the only family she has left. Because of that, she's always had a soft spot for us; always wanting to help fix things regardless of whether we want the help or not, but then, that's what siblings are for I suppose.

The problem is she knows, like really knows, too fucking much about my past. Thanks for that, Finn. When she gives me that look, I just know she's thinking of . . . well, that; and wanting to help fix things for me. Really, it's fine. . . I'm beyond fixing anyway.

"Oh, nothing much. Was bored so I thought I'd call and check in with you guys. How are things going, anyway? Giovanni mentioned a kid down the hall; you watching Wolfie again tonight?"

Danni's grin is ecstatic at the mention of her godson, Wolfie. I've never had the chance to meet him in person, or his mom for that matter. During the season, I'm always too busy with my game schedule, and during the summer months my visits have always seemed misaligned with their own schedules.

But I've seen Wolfie on the phone many times. Cute kid. He's not much of a talker, but he reminds me a lot of Finn when we were younger. He's slowly warmed up to me over the last several years, whenever I would have video chats with Danni on the nights when he stayed over at her place. I know she had been really disappointed when he had to stop staying over during the last several months.

Danni had been dealing with a stalker situation off and on for years that unfortunately escalated after I pushed her into coming to my game and reconnecting with Theo. Turns out her stalker was the same person who had been blackmailing my boy T for years, and ultimately the one responsible for keeping them apart for so long. But when the threats escalated, it became clear the situation was no longer safe enough for her godson to stay at her place for their weekly sleepovers, like she had had with him in the past.

"Yeah, Wolfie is staying with us for a few days." Danica's voice is quiet, but her joy at having him back over is undeniable as it lights up her whole face. "QT is taking a few personal days that are way overdue after everything that's been going on. She had to go out of town to deal with some things, your neck of the woods actually, so I figured what better opportunity than now to have Wolfie over again? After all, my stalker situation is all cleared up finally, and Theo has been incredible in prepping this dream house of ours. It has practically everything we could ever want or need; and really, between Theo, Jay and Finn, they were able to prepare a room for Wolfie in no time at all. It's so great to have him here, in our home. It feels unreal, almost."

Oh geeze, now I know that's not Theo getting all glassy-eyed over there at her dropping the words 'our home.' I really have to fight back the eye roll this time.

"That's neither here nor there, though. I know you weren't just calling because you were bored after your big win tonight. And you also weren't calling to hear me raving about having my adorable godson back under my roof. So what's going on? For real this time." Danica gives me a pointed look and I bite back a grimace.

"Damn, Kitty Cat. Those claws are sharp tonight."

"Oh shut it. I'm not even being mean, so much as calling it like I see it. Now stop dancing around the subject. What's going on?"

I shrug, trying to find the words. "Dunno. .. I just. . . feel kinda . . . off, I guess? I've been feeling it the last few weeks but it hit me hard tonight. Going out with the guys just wasn't it for me, but I can't seem to shut my mind off or focus on anything else. I figured calling and saying 'hi' wouldn't be a bad thing, but I didn't realize I would be. . . interrupting, either."

Danica's face softens, as recognition lights her eyes. And there it is. She always has been too intuitive when it comes to Finn and I.

"You can interrupt us anytime, we're always here for you." Her voice is gentle as she responds.

"Speak for yourself, I was having a damn good time before he interrupted." Theo's grumble is cut off with a dull thud as she playfully smacks at his chest. His expression is sullen, and I swear I can hear his muffled "Ow!" as he subtly rubs his chest, but there's no mistaking the amusement in his eyes as he looks at Danni. "Really?"

A smile pulls at the corner of my lips as I see him pretend to glower at her.

"Don't be rude. Of course you can call and interrupt us any time. We're always here for you. Especially today."

The inflection of her tone as she emphasizes 'today' makes me wince. Yep. Today. The day I dread the most each year. December twenty-first. Normally,I would already be in Washington by now, with my brother and closest friends celebrating what little time I have off around the holidays. It has become a tradition of mine, but it helps keep the dark thoughts at bay. This year, our game schedule didn't allow for me to fly out early, so I have to wait until Sunday morning to catch a flight.

"Are you still coming over for Christmas?" Danica's tone is hopeful as she interrupts my spiraling thoughts.

"Yep. Just like always. Only better this time, since we are finally getting the whole band back together. It will be great to be able to celebrate with everyone all in one spot this year."

Now it's Danni and Theo who are wincing. Over the last six years since their separation, our Christmas holiday has been split like that of kids being shuffled between parents during a custody battle, splitting half our time with Theo and the other half with Danica so the two never had to interact.

For the first time in way too long, we're all going together for Christmas. Theo spent the time they were apart focused on building the house of Danica's dreams with the hope that one day they would share it together; so now they have a home large enough to host all of their closest friends and family all under one roof for the holiday celebrations.

"Oh! And you can finally meet QT and Wolfie in person! Plus, I think Sierra is actually going to make it this year with Connor." There is a slightly sour look on her face as she says his name. "I could do without Connor, but we haven't seen Sierra in forever, so if she's able to come, even if it's only for a day or two, that would be so incredible! Gosh, I can't wait for all of my favorite people to finally be together for the holidays!"

"Yeah, it's gonna be great." My voice is more withdrawn than I intended, and I think she notices.

"Hey, are you sure you can't come earlier?"

"Nah." I shake my head. "Flights were all pretty full, the earliest I could get was for Sunday.

Originally, I had been scheduled for an earlier flight to Seattle, but due to inclement weather, one of our away games ended up getting rescheduled to tonight, which in turn, pushed back my being able to fly out. And because my original flight had been booked months ago, it was damn near impossible to get a new ticket booked on such short notice right before Christmas.

"You do realize your twin has his own private jet thanks to his company, don't you? You could literally fly out any time you wanted." Theo gives me a pointed look and I have to fight the urge to flip him off. "Not to mention that you are part owner in said company, which has allowed him to purchase it in the first place? Therefore said jet technically belongs to you as well."

"Yeah, well," I shrug, waving him off dismissively. "You know me. I don't need anything that fancy. Besides, why tie it up for my own future use? You never know when Finn's gonna have another work emergency which requires its use?" I bend my fingers in air quotes as I say this, my tone only slightly sarcastic.

It's not an unknown fact that my twin has had several rather mysterious 'work emergencies' over the last few months which have tied him up. Hell, he was so busy with these 'emergencies' that it even took away from his being able to focus on Danni and Theo's case, which is completely unheard of for him. I tried asking him about it on several occasions but he is being unusually tight-lipped about the whole thing.

"Besides, I have plans that I can't get out of for tomorrow." With a shrug, I brush away any wistful thoughts at the idea of commandeering the Erebus jet to fly me out sooner. Okay, so what if I don't really have plans preventing me from coming to visit sooner. They don't need to know that.

"Anyway, I guess I should let you guys get back to it." Plastering a cheesy grin on my face, I waggle my eyebrows in an exaggerated manner, my tone full of barely disguised innuendo. My former roommate just gives me an unamused glare, but Danni blushes so much that I can see it through the dim lighting on the screen, though she grins back at me anyway.

"Bash!"

"Dude, seriously?"

"Later!" I chuckle, hanging up on them before they can circle back to the topic of me flying out early. Tossing my phone on the table once more, I glance again at the tv screen, before looking over to the clock on the far wall. Shit. As amusing as that conversation was, it really didn't eat up all that much time. Guess I'm gonna have to find something else to distract me.

"Rhea, what's on my social calendar for tonight?"

"Alright, let me check your social calendar." The digitized female voice of the virtual assistant program Finn set up for me echoes throughout the quiet room. "Friday, December Twenty-First, ten p.m. Rocky marathon on CenturyOne. Eleven p.m. possible game celebration. Eleven p.m. Candy Cane Masquerade at Sintuary off of Orchid Lane. You have four unopened notifications on Quasi. You have twelve unread-"

"Rhea, stop."

Immediately, the monotonous tone halts.

Without a second thought, I am leaning over once more to grab my phone and quickly scroll through my email until I find the link.

Sintuary, the exclusive club that I've been a member of for the last few years, is holding their annual holiday masquerade party tonight. I completely forgot. And I think I know exactly what I need to help me out of my funk.

# Chapter Three

## Bash

**"H**i, baby. Are you looking for some fun tonight?"
Talon-like nails brush across my chest, in what's supposed to be an enticing manner, as a woman's voice whispers in my ear from behind. The cloyingly sweet smell of coconut and vanilla waft around me and I bristle at the familiarity of her words.

"Monique."

The willowy brunette slowly circles me, the click of her sharp stilettos audibly noticeable even over the erotic melody coming from the stage off to one side. Not deterred by my lack of warmth to her less than subtle greeting, her hand continues to glide across my back and shoulders, nails grazing with the slightest edge. As she comes to stand before me, unashamed of her brazen appearance, I give her a quick once-over, a bored perusal of what she is offering blatantly. I may not be attracted to the viper, but I'm not blind either.

At 5'9" she is on the shorter side for a model in the industry, but what she lacks in height she's always made up for with her killer looks and she knows it. Unfortunately, she's always had a venomous attitude to match. And she has had her eyes set on me for months. I would say she's a wolf in sheep's clothing but given the fact that she is wearing nothing but stilettos and. . .

"Santa hat nipple pasties?" Quirking an eyebrow, I glance up in time to see the indecorous grin she must mean to be seductive.

"Mmm. Do you like them?" Biting her lip playfully, she leans closer, running her hands slowly down my chest. "I picked them out just for you."

"Now, now. Monique."

Grabbing her by the wrists, I halt her hands on their journey before they can travel any lower, their bawdy exploration already boldly toying with the waistband of my slacks.

Sidestepping her question, I continue. "Gotta watch those hands of yours. Wouldn't want to make me feel like you're only after me for my . . . charming personality, now. Would you?"

I tsk in feigned disappointment, trying to mentally block out her hyena laugh, as I glance subtly around the room; causally searching for another poor libertine on whom I could pawn off her bold advances without her noticing.

"Baby," her whining is supposed to come off playful, cutesy even, but it just continues to grate on my nerves and I have to fight back the annoyance. Maybe it wasn't such a good idea to come here after all. "Come play with me."

My hands are still locked around her wrists, preventing her from grabbing at me, and she switches tactics, leaning forward to brush her santa-hat nipple tits against my chest as she stands on tiptoes, licking up my neck. "Don't you want me to make you feel better?"

I'm not one to turn down the advances of a beautiful woman often; God knows I've had more than my fair share over the years, and have been called a player for more than just my moves on the ice, yet I feel nothing but annoyance as this statuesque beauty rubs herself all over me. I stiffen, glancing anywhere else but here as I try futilely to redirect the advances of the woman now clinging to me like a koala and from across the room, something catches my eye.

A dark-haired goddess, looking completely out of place in the best possible way, sits at the bar alone. . . as if waiting for me. Looking bored out of her mind, chin resting on one hand as she holds a drink in the other, her black painted nails tapping against the side of her glass as her unimpressed gaze takes in the room.

Her features are striking. Deliciously thick, tan curves covered in tattoos are framed by her black lace corset, and ebony hair pulled back off her face, the red ribbon holding it in place and matching red boots her only nod to tonight's holiday theme. Our eyes meet, and a jolt of awareness shoots through me like lightning, sending chills along my suddenly overheated skin. One corner of her mouth pulls up, the faintest hint of amusement shining through her otherwise unimpressed features as she glances from me, to the forgotten stage-five clinger dangling from my neck.

Just like that, a shadow of something passes over her features, twisting my gut. *What put that sad look on your face, gorgeous girl?* Gone before I can decipher its meaning, so fast that I am second-guessing what I saw, she once again dons an expression of boredom, raising a sardonic eyebrow in my direction before looking away with disinterest. What felt like an electric connection, a depth of familiarity I don't know how to fully register, is gone in seconds. Disappointment sits like a lead weight on my chest.

"Oh, you like that baby?" The pale blonde croons in my ear, pulling me back to the present. Swallowing thickly, I reluctantly drag my gaze away from my dark vixen.

"No, Monica." Shifting my hands from her wrists, I take hold of her shoulders, careful not to let my fingers brush anywhere that could imply interest, and move her backwards. She peels off of me like gum clinging to hot pavement, her exaggerated pout one that would make weaker men beg. But I'm not a weak man. Not for her. "I really don't."

"It's Monique - "

Stepping around her, her indignant protests fall on deaf ears as my gaze zones back in on my dark temptress, and I'm frozen on the spot. Charles fucking Landry is talking to my girl. Not just talking to her, he's eye-fucking her with his leering gaze. I can practically see him licking his sweaty wrinkled lips from over here.

An icy rage fills me, that the perve would dare to even approach someone so perfect, so exquisitely luscious and taint her with his simpering limp-dicked presence has me fuming. Gone is my good-natured, rational self, left in its place is a man I don't recognize; One who could rip the wrinkly balls right off the bastard and shove them down the old man's throat simply for making near her.

Quickly, I assess the situation, noting how she shifts uncomfortably on the stool, her gaze flicking past him, looking for a way out of what has to be an incredibly awkward conversation. Forcing a calm I no longer feel, I shove down the explosion of emotions that have taken me by storm, throwing off my equilibrium. It's time I officially introduce myself to my girl.

Hello
Sunshine

# Chapter Four

## Quincy

**A**fter showing my exclusive invite, my ID, verifying my identity with a fingerprint scan and then turning in my clutch with my phone to the attendant on the first level, I was finally admitted into the inner levels of Sintuary. A club notorious for hosting some of the hottest celebrities in the world, with four locations (Calgary being the founding location, with branches that later opened in New York City, Los Angeles and Paris) I still don't know how Sierra managed to swing an exclusive invitation, especially to one of their member-only parties.

My understanding is that the base membership price is around twenty thousand dollars a year, but the more exclusive tiers range closer to a cool million. It's no wonder that the majority of speculated members range from movie stars to politicians. With events like these? Even for members, the tickets are highly exclusive. And for guests of pass holders, there is an extensive vetting process, complete with background checks and a lot of legal paperwork. I had to sign an NDA before I could even get information on the date or theme of the event.

My eyes widen as I step off the elevator playing sensual cello music. I don't know what I was expecting, but it certainly wasn't this. The room is bright; white marble floors match the pristine white counter of the bar. The bar stools are more of a gray-marble coloring but look to have plush cushion seats. Chandeliers hang from the high vaulted ceiling, reflecting their luminescent glow from the genuine crystals. The walls, while not white, are a textured pattern in soft grays that compliment and give warmth to the bright room.

In contrast, milling about are dozens of glammed-up women in various shades of crimson red. A well-known actress in a blood-red minidress; an heiress often gossiped about in the tabloids is wearing a sparkling red bra and miniskirt, stilettos sky-high and her lips coated in a frosty white glitter. And I'm pretty sure I just saw a supermodel wearing nothing more than Santa hat nipple pasties walk past me just now.

Quickly, I do a double-take. Yep, those were definitely Santa hat themed nipple pasties. Fluffy white just barely covered the nipple, while the pasties themselves were shaped like the sparkly red cone of a Santa hat.

Out of habit, I run a self-conscious hand over my curvy front. Much more curvy. Holy shit. I could be at least two of these other women combined. That wasn't kind. I'm sure they are all lovely women. But seriously. I look like I ate one of them. My plus-size tan complexioned, tattooed figure is so out of place in a setting like this.

Unlike the myriad of women milling about, laughing with fake grins plastered on their faces and drinks in their hands dressed in various shades of sparkling crimson (or not dressed at all), the men in the room (much fewer in number, I might add) are all dressed the same. Black top, black pants and shoes. Crimson red bow tie. And the mask of course. Everyone is wearing some sort of mask tonight. With that, I breathe a sigh of relief. It doesn't matter that I am clearly like ten sizes bigger than the other women here (seriously, is nobody in this room above a size two?) Nor does it matter that I am all curves and covered in tattoos, which make me stick out like a sore thumb.

Because, just like the rest of the women here, I have my mask on. My mask is my secret identity. I can be anyone I choose tonight. I can do things I wouldn't allow myself to normally do or think or feel or say. I am a brand new me in this room tonight. And this is a new role that I am nervous to play.

"You come here often?"

Sitting at the bar, drink in hand, I turn to face the voice behind me, reluctantly pulling my gaze away from the gorgeous man across the room. Our gazes had met from across the way while I was nursing my favorite non-alcoholic cocktail and trying to pretend like I belong here. And in an instant, it was as if no one else was in the room, my pulse racing from the intense scrutiny of his gaze. That is, until I noticed the bleach-blonde stunner with the nipple tassels from earlier plastered to his front.

"Ahem," With effort, I shift my attention back to the man sitting next to me. I forgot what he said already. Shit. Greasy, thinning gray hair and leering eyes gape openly at my chest, the mask does nothing to hide the lascivious glance as he gives me slow once-over. Nor does the sparkly red tie which aims to be festive take away from his discomforting attention.

"Uh-" I'm unsure of how to answer, uncomfortable with his attention and completely uncaring of what his question had been.

"We could, you know. . .go downstairs. Have some fun, if you know what I mean?" The man licks his lips, actually licks his lips as he reaches out to touch my breast through the fabric of my top.

"Oh. . . um. No, thank you. I'm-" My voice starts to crack, but I clear my throat, pushing on in as confident a manner as I can. "I'm actually waiting for my partner."

"Partner, you say?" A sheen of sweat is breaking across the older man's wrinkly forehead, and his hand stretches to reach for me once more, though I manage to turn my body just in time and he grabs a handful of my shoulder rather than the breast he had been aiming for. "A partner could be fun. Tell me, do they like to watch?"

Very uncomfortably, I try my best to shift out of his grasp, but the hand tightens, almost painfully and I can't seem to get away fast enough.

"Well-"

"There you are. Sorry I'm late, Sunshine." A light kiss on my cheek sends shockwaves spiraling through me as I am bombarded by the scent of leather and spice. It's him. I don't know how I know it, I don't even have to look to know that it's the mystery man from across the room. He's here. He called me Sunshine. Wait, he called me what? Heat spreads across my cheeks as butterflies fill me with the hand that reaches to flatten across my stomach, and a solid warmth presses into my back sending all the racing thoughts right out of my head.

"You're her partner?" The older gentleman's hand drops from my shoulder, and he gawps openly at the man who has just come to my rescue. As if the nasty old man can't possibly believe that whoever is behind me could actually be my partner.

"That's right, Landry. And you know I don't share what's mine." The voice behind me which had been full of warmth mere seconds ago is now ice-cold, and it's a wonder the creepy man standing before me isn't frozen on the spot.

"No, no. You're right. Of course not. I'm sorry, my friend. No offense meant by it."

He speaks as if I am not even here now, eyes blatantly looking in any direction but my own; which is almost funny, considering how they had been leering at me before my mystery man came to the rescue.

"None taken, unless you don't clear out. I need some privacy with my girl."

"Of course, of course. Will I see you both at the fundraiser on the 30th?"

Mystery man gives no response at first, and I shift uncomfortably as the older man's eyes roam back to leer longingly at me once more.

I can't see his face, but the mystery man's hand tightens imperceptibly, almost protectively across my abdomen, pulling me in closer as a low-rumbled, "I'll be there," fills the awkward silence. For a moment, no one speaks, but the creepy older man standing before me pulls uncomfortably at his sparkly red tie before giving a brief nod and turning to leave in the opposite direction.

With a sigh of relief, I turn to face the mystery man as my shoulders loosen from their tensed posture.

"Thank you for that." I nod my head backwards, in the general direction that I last saw Mr. Creep-Head.

"You looked like you could use a helping hand."

My breath catches in my throat as I am hit by the close-up view of this Adonis standing before me. He is tall, has to be at least 6 '3". Dark, wavy hair, just a little too long as it brushes the tops of his ears, and a chiseled body with muscles that are practically bursting out of his fitted black button-down.

In opposition to the rest of the men wandering the festive room, he wears a standard red tie done in a simple knot, rather than what must be the dress-code standard of the sparkly red number everyone else is wearing. A simple black mask hides most of his face, but it can't hide his gorgeous honey-colored eyes with lines just crinkling the edges. Nor does it take away from the well-cut beard. That must have been what was tickling my face. And there is something about him. . . so familiar. But I swear I've never met him before.

"I'm sorry, what?"

Belatedly, I realize the man kept speaking while my thoughts were drifting over his fine body. I completely missed whatever it was he just said.

A smile breaks across his face, and the crinkles at the corners of his eyes deepen slightly, even as his pearly whites glisten under the lavish chandelier lighting.

"I was just asking if you were okay?"

"Oh, um. . ." I smooth a hand down the front of my top once more. Damn, that really is a habit that I need to break. "Yeah, thanks. I was actually just getting ready to head out."

He cocks his head, as if considering me.

"Now, why would you go and do a thing like that?"

"Oh, well. . . you know." I shrug, feigning nonchalance. "Not a whole lot going on here. Figured I'd call it a night." This gorgeous god of a man does not need to know that for the past hour I have been sitting here, babying my drink while I have been passed over time and again for women who were skinnier and . . . blonder. . . than me. I wasn't lying either. I was just about ready to call it quits. And technically I did come to a sex club, and participate in conversations, so I definitely think it counts towards crossing this one off my bucket list. It took a lot of cajones (as Jay would say) just for me to stick it out over the last hour, and I'm damn proud of myself for that fact

Though it's hard to read his expression, between the beard and the mask, his honey eyes continue to stare intently back at me as we sit in silence. It's not awkward, and strangely enough not uncomfortable like the silence of a few moments before with

Mr. Creep. But it does feel. . . encompassing. As if the world around me has faded to gray and nothing else matters outside of that liquid gold in his eyes.

"Have a drink with me." It wasn't a question.

"No, thanks. I'm good.." I lift the drink I have been babying, tipping back the glass and downing the last excuse I had to remain in this seat. "I really do think I'm gonna call it a night." Setting down the now empty drinkware, out of habit I find myself reaching for my clutch before remembering belatedly that I had to check it with the attendant on the entry-floor.

"Please." He gestures for me to resume my seat at the bar, before pulling up another stool close to me. "I insist." There's an intensity to his words that belies the smile crinkling the corners of his eyes as he smiles back at me.

Hesitation wars with my unexpected attraction. I glance from his hand which is still gesturing for me to resume sitting, up to his face. While his tone was commanding, underneath that I sense an earnestness in his gaze, something deeper, almost pleading about his look that he doesn't want me to see. I should be nervous. I should just follow my gut and go home. Because I have a gnawing feeling that this man could ruin me and the curious part of me is dying to find out what that would be like.

He must see the wavering of my determination, because the hand that had been at his side gently comes up to the middle of my back, guiding me back to resume my seat.

"What'll you have, Sunshine?" Oh good. A simple question. I can answer this.

"A Roy Rogers."

His brows raise in surprise, but he flags down the bartender nearest to where we are seated. "Two Roy Rogers' please. On my tab." The bartender nods, before turning to make our drinks. "So, a Roy Rogers huh?"

"You didn't have to get the same drink as me." I don't bother going into details with him about why I am choosing a non-alcoholic beverage. For tonight, I am just another woman out on the town, not Wolfie's mom and full-time caregiver needing to keep her wits about her. For all this guy knows, maybe I am a recovering alcoholic. Or maybe I just like the taste of mocktails better. Oh god, there my anxious thoughts go again. Get it together, Quincy. You are a fierce, gorgeous bitch. You've got this. But what if he thinks I'm weird for getting a mocktail? What if -

"I know." That's all he says in response.

Hello
Stranger

# Chapter Five

## Bash

**"S**o, Miss Roy Rogers. What is your favorite book?"

I bite back a smirk as she chokes on her drink, coughing in an ungraceful manner. Her nose crinkles, a look of confusion crossing her gorgeous face. Rather than making her less attractive, it simply adds to her charm. Unlike a lot of the women in this room tonight, the curvy vixen before me clearly hasn't leaned on the use of cosmetic enhancements to remove any perceived imperfections. God forbid a woman show laugh lines or any real signs of emotions on her face. It's a refreshing change.

With all of the puck bunnies and models I have been with in the past, it's never even registered on my radar. But now, with this natural beauty sitting before me, it's hard not to notice the glaring difference. Harder still, not to find every other woman in this room lacking by comparison. Plus, I have to admit, the confused look and the way she wrinkles her nose at me is kinda cute on her. Surprise hits me in the gut as I find myself having to fight the urge not to lean over and kiss the bridge of her nose where it crinkles. There will be time for that later.

"I'm sorry?"

"I asked, what is your favorite book?"

Her eyes are pools of liquid chocolate against the lace of her mask as they swirl with curiosity. Her face lights up at the question, though she quickly tries to hide it. I can't help but watch as she chews on her luscious lips, considering her response. Soon it will be me that gets to take a bite out of her full, pouty mouth. My cock stiffens at the thought and I shift, trying to subtly readjust myself. No need to overwhelm her with my intentions . . .yet.

"I'm sorry, your question caught me off guard. I was expecting a simple 'what brings you here tonight?' or the ever-cliche 'what's your sign, tell me yours and I'll tell you mine, blah blah blah.' Why the book question? It's not the stereotypical pick-up line I would have expected from a g-"

Interesting. Is she deliberately evading the question?

"What? From a guy like me, you mean?" I can't help but smirk at that. "Does this mean that you assume I came over here to try and hook up with you? That seems a bit presumptuous, wouldn't you think?" And altogether wrong. I want so much more from you than a simple fuck and flee, gorgeous. "Maybe I just came over here to save you from another uncomfortable ten minutes of dealing with 'Lewd' Landry before you were able to escape on your own. I should be offended that you think so little of me, that I would have to resort to those tactics."

My tone is teasing as I say it. I mean, she's not entirely wrong. I absolutely am that guy that would normally look for an easy fuck with no strings attached. But there's something about her that is drawing me into her gravity. Something exotic and thrilling. A tangible connection that I haven't felt since losing . . . well, no need to think about that now.

Besides, I do have every intention of being that guy. The lucky son of a bitch that gets to taste every inch of her delicate curves. Though I have no intention of making this a one time thing. Not with dark radiance pulling me into her gravity. Still, she doesn't know that is what I was coming over here for. For all she knows, I could be a damn cub scout here to simply rescue her from Charles Landry and the fucker's roving hands.

No woman should have to suffer the miserable fate of being trapped in conversation with him, between his lewd comments, sleazy gaze and roving hands. I would have stepped in for any woman I saw looking uncomfortable in his presence. The fact that he set his predatory gaze on my fucking ray of sunshine in this den of sin? Well that was just unacceptable. Still, it gave me an easy excuse to cut in, anyway. Not that it mattered. One way or another, we were always going to end up right here, like this. It was kismet.

"Tell you what. I'll answer your question if you answer mine first."

Those beautiful lips form a thoughtful pout as she considers my offer, and not even a hint of remorse at making a rash judgement about my character. Very interesting, indeed.

"Okay. But, just remember, you asked for this. So you'd better brace yourself." Her reluctance gives way to a mischievous grin, and my heart skips a fucking beat. Literally skips like a goddamn pebble on water. I thought she was gorgeous before but holy fuck. Having that radiant joy and playfulness directed at me? I am a lucky man indeed.

I have to bite back a smile as her expression turns serious once more. There was something about her that told me she wouldn't go for the normal advance. Taking a play out of Danni's playbook, I lean hard into our past discussions to look for a more interesting ice breaker, and from the joy written all throughout her body language, even with the now serious expression on her face, clearly I guessed correctly.

"Off the top of my head, my favorite books include, but are not limited to: Shattered Lights, The Morning After, and A Referendum of Fears and Salutations. My favorite authors - in no particular order, I might add- include Shann McPherson, SJ Tilly, H.D. Carlton, and Shantiel Tessier. I have a deep-rooted love for all things dark romance, fantasy and rom-coms, but will also enjoy a good biography or manga when the mood strikes."

I go to respond, but she cuts me off, continuing.

"Along with this, I am also an avid reader of medical journals and assorted research literature.

My mouth opens, then closes once more. Huh. Not what I was expecting. *Okay, I can work with this.*

"Now. I answered your question. Remember, no judgments. Please return the favor."

"Sure." I grin widely. "I'll have you know, I am also a huge fan of Shann McPherson's works." Her jaw drops in shock and I continue. "No judgement, remember?"

Her stunned expression makes me chuckle.

"N- not judging. I swear! Just surprised, is all. I haven't met too many men that willingly admit they like a good smutty rom-com, be it novel or movie. Not saying there aren't plenty out there that do, just that I haven't personally met many willing to openly admit it to a complete stranger."

"But we aren't strangers, are we Sunshine?" I shoot her a wink as I continue, but she just rolls her eyes in response. "Besides, ain't no shame in my reading game. I had a friend point out to me a while back that these romance novels women seem to love so much are practically a guide to giving a woman exactly what they want. A 'how-to' guide, if you will. Now, I'm not saying I didn't have game before, but by expanding my world a bit. I'd like to think that I gained some insight into the inner workings of the female mind."

She chokes, coughing on the drink that she swallowed wrong, and for a moment I am mesmerized by the bobbing of her throat and her watery eyes. My mind circles straight down the drain and I have to shift in my seat, subtly adjusting my dick once more. It had been hard since I first spotted her from across the room, but now with every passing minute spent in her company it's quickly becoming painfully uncomfortable.

"Inner workings of the female mind, you say?" Soft, dainty fingers wipe delicately at the slightly smudged makeup, and I have to fight back thoughts of seeing that makeup streak down her pretty face as she chokes on my cock.

"Yes, ma'am." My nod is sure, and she cocks her head to the side curiously at my response.

"Please, do tell." Is that sarcasm dripping from her tone? She almost sounds annoyed at my answer. "And don't call me, 'ma'am'. Makes me sound like I'm old." Her nose crinkles in disgust as she says the word and I have to bite back another laugh.

"Well, you see, whether you are wanting to read a book with a golden retriever boyfriend, or one that is dripping with blood left behind by all the waving red flags, there is always a common element to the books that draws the women, one that men can learn from." I pause, momentarily, letting my words sink in.

"Obsession. The men in these stories are obsessed with their women. They may be complete assholes who want to burn down the world, and sure, they may all have giant dicks and know how to fuck their women into oblivion, but at the end of the day, the men all treat their women like the fucking goddesses they are."

I have her attention now, her eyes widening in surprise at my words.

"Ah! See!" My grin is wide as it spreads across my face, and I point a teasing finger in her direction. "You thought I was gonna say that women read the books for the men with the big dicks that know how to fuck. Admit it."

I can see the wheels spinning in her head, this gorgeous woman has no poker face, even with her mask on. Definitely not the type of woman who usually haunts a place like this. My gaze catches once more on her pursed lips as she nods slowly, before grinning back at me.

"Alright, yes, fine. I totally had you pegged for one of those frat guys who only thinks about sex." Leaning closer, she gestures in a 'come hither' motion as if she wants to tell me a secret, so I bend my tall frame, moving closer to her decadent mouth.

"I mean, we are in an exclusive sex club, after all." With that, she lifts her drink and sips slowly and it takes everything in me not to lean forward and lick the drop of cocktail clinging to her pouty lip before claiming her mouth with my own.

"Well sure, that is a draw for reading the stories. Hell, I'll admit a lot of those scenes are hot as fuck. But honestly, at the end of the day, women just want their book boyfriends to be the hero that thinks his woman is his whole world. So why not take a few notes from the experts on how to make women feel like fucking royalty?"

I shrug. It's not like it isn't true. I still remember the first time I teased Danni for reading her smut books, but she called me out on my 'typical male frat-boy shit' and dared me to read one of her books; practically threw it at my face, actually. But I did end up reading it, and it changed my dating life for the better.

I'm no saint, and I sure as hell won't ever win a 'boyfriend of the year' award. That would require sticking around for more than a few dates. But in the time I do spend with these women, I make them feel like they are the only woman in my world; because while we are together, they are.

"So you mean to tell me, that you aren't like every other rich, stuck-up asshole in here, looking for some easy pussy before he bails?" One eyebrow arches as she eyes me skeptically, her tone dripping with sarcasm.

"Oh honey, I'm exactly like the other rich assholes in this room tonight." Or at least I have been. Until tonight. Until her. "The only difference is, I know how to take care of my woman." And she may not know it yet, but she is mine. I throw back the rest of my drink, then grimace slightly at the sweetness, remembering belatedly that it is not my go-to Macallan, but a fucking Roy Rogers.

"Come with me." Standing, I extend my hand to help her up.

Not bothering with subtlety, she hesitates, giving me a long once over before she places her small hand in mine, and hops off the seat. Her fucking mouthwatering tits bounce slightly within the confines of her tightly laced black and red corset and her cheeks flush under the heat of my gaze. Stepping away from the bar, I lace her delicate fingers through my own rough ones, and internally cringe at my calluses rubbing against her silky-smooth skin.

She moves to follow me, and as she steps closer to my side, I use the opportunity to fully take her in. Jesus, she's tiny, she barely comes up to my chest. Unlike the other women circulating the modestly lit room, she isn't rail thin. Shiny, black hair tied back with a silk red ribbon, corset made of fine black lacework stands in contrast to her bronze skin which is covered in an intricate design of tattoos, highlighting her luscious curves.

Every other woman in this place pales in comparison. Their

ruby-red scantily clad attire clashing violently against this woman's more subtle and alluring charm. A vixen. A nymph. A goddess in the night. And now? She's all mine.

"Holy shit, you're tall!" Her words come out loud and unfiltered, and her whole face turns as red as some of the outfits spread throughout the room.

# Chapter Six

## *Quincy*

**"H**oly shit, you're tall!" Taking the hand that he offers, I am in awe of his beauty as I move closer to where he stands before me. He's staring at me with a heated look in his eyes. Oh fuck. Did I just say that out loud? My face flames with mortification and I groan. "Oh, god. I'm sorry. Ignore me. I have a bad habit of just blurting things out sometimes." And now, I must look like a simpering airhead to him.

He grins, shaking his head as he gently tugs, leading me forward.

"Come on."

I don't know where he's taking me, and quite frankly, at the moment I just don't care. All I can focus on is the tingling awareness where our hands are joined and the aching desire now pulsing through my veins in time to the beat of my frantic heart.

A sea of red scantily-clad women parts before him as he guides me through the crowd to the back of the room. Another bouncer is standing silently at a door I hadn't noticed before, but the man just nods in silent greeting before moving to the side to let us through.

The bright white and soft grays of the room behind us give way to a dimly lit hall, covered in thick, plush padding in darker shades.  After walking a short way, the mystery man holding my hand turns to the side, opening another door and the dark gray tones give way to moody lighting and black covered walls as we make our way down a long set of stairs. We pass a couple that are openly fucking against the wall, one man leaning against the railing for support while the other man pounds into him from behind, their loud moans of pleasure causing heat to flood my cheeks. Oh god, I am so out of my element here. This is nothing like what I have done in the past. Not even with Mistress Simone the few times she and I role-played together.

I quickly avert my gaze, but not before I catch the smirk of my masked adonis leading me further into the darkness. As our eyes meet, his smirk gives way to a full-on cocky grin.

"You don't come here often, I take it?"

I laugh sharply, my response clipped.

"Gee, whatever would make you think that?"

He doesn't respond though, just shaking his head in silent amusement as he continues forward, leading me down a much darker hallway at the foot of the stairs.

It is much less crowded down here, but loud moans and shrieks of pleasure fill the air. My breath catches in my throat as I realize that these rooms on either side of us have large windows for the viewing pleasure of passersby. Some are blacked out, only muffled grunts and sounds of slapping skin coming from behind closed doors. For others, the rooms are brightly illuminated behind clear glass for all to see.

One room we pass appears to be having an all-out orgy, and I can't help myself as I stop and stare, fascinated, at the three men pleasuring the woman who is literally tied up in a complicated-looking series of knots and hanging from the ceiling.

My head cocks to the side as I take in the sight before me, my own body flushing with heat at the exhibition in the window. The woman is tied up and hanging from the ceiling at the height-level of the bed in some sort of complicated looking swing-thing, while one man fucks her mouth and another fucks her from behind. A third man is beneath them, on his knees, his face buried in her pussy, eating her out.

"You like that, Sunshine?" I jump, biting back a shriek at the voice whispering in my ear.

"Jesus, you scared me!" I turn my back on the view, lightly smacking mystery-man's shoulder.

Letting go of my hand, he gently grabs me around the waist, and turns me back to the view once more. Large hands slide across my abdomen, and I am pulled tight against his warm body, his breath whispering across my ear.

"Look at those men. Watch how they're taking care of their woman." One hand glides up, slowly, a lazy caress over my bodice before lightly wrapping his warm fingers around the base of my neck. Fingers circle me in warmth as he reaches with his thumb to tilt my head up, and I shiver as his mouth lightly skims across the shell of my ear before he speaks once more.

"Three men fucking her. You would think it was for their own pleasure, but look at her face. Can you see heaven written all over her body? The flushed tone of her skin? The stars reflected in her eyes as they roll back in ecstasy from those men filling her completely?"

A light nip on my earlobe, and I breathe in sharply, before a light trail of kisses down my neck leaves me covered in goosebumps. The hand around my throat squeezes lightly, while his other hand trails down my body in slow, lazy circles, inching lower until it brushes the smooth skin of my thigh.

"You like that? Watching those men fill her up? Or is it the woman bound, giving over all control that fascinates you?"

Another soft nip against my neck as his fingers trail under my skirt. My skin is overheated, and I have to bite back a breathless moan as his fingers brush against my center.

"You like the idea of being tied up? Of giving all control to your partner? There's a certain level of trust in allowing yourself to be  bound or blindfolded, in giving up yourself so completely to another."

He licks from my collar bone to my ear, his fingers finding their way to my pussy, the crotchless panties giving him full access beneath my corset.

"Jesus!" My breathing is ragged now, and I can't help it as my eyes close, lost in the foreign feeling of fullness as his finger thrusts into me while his thumb teases my clit.

"Eyes open, honey. Keep watching."

"Oh!"

My eyes shoot open when he adds more pressure with his thumb. Circling more deliberately, I bite down hard on my lip, trying desperately to hold back a lust-filled moan as he adds a second finger inside, thrusting in and out of me. He nips my earlobe once more, and I can't help the breathy sigh that escapes me.

"Mmm. That's a good girl. You like to watch, don't you? See that one there, fucking her mouth? It's not just about his big dick filling her up; watch his hands. Watch how he teases one nipple, giving it his full attention even as he caresses the side of her face."

His fingers start to fuck me with a more consistent rhythm, stretching me. His rough callouses add a delicious friction that has my body flushing with heat even as my arousal drips down his fingers.

"And the man standing behind her? Sure, he's fucking her ass, stretching her and filling her up. But look at the way he pulls back on her hair, the way he squeezes her throat and then releases it with measured deliberation? When they come together, she is going to explode with the pleasure of the tension in her head releasing, and the endorphins rushing into her after the breath play."

My own breath catches once more, as he adds a third finger, stretching me further, my body feeling impossibly full.

"Mmm. You do like that, my naughty little minx. I can feel your body, sucking me in. Your pussy is practically begging for me to come and play."

His hand tightens on my throat, squeezing gently as he trails more kisses back down the side of my neck.

"But the real star of the show? That is happening even lower. Look down, little minx. A man can fuck a woman a million different ways, but there is nothing so sweet, so deliciously dirty, as a man getting on his knees to worship his woman."

He pauses his words, sucking hard on the side of my neck, tongue trailing an intricate pattern before he bites, this time a sharp sting in contrast to the soft, playful nips from before. As he does so, his thumb stops circling my clit to press firmly, and I gasp at the intrusion as he pumps a fourth digit inside, stretching me impossibly wide.

I can't help it. The fullness. The needy ache in my center even as he fills me with his calloused touch;  I press my back into his chest, desperate for more, and his grip on my neck tightens ever so slightly, stars dancing around the edge of my vision. And then, I shatter.

"Oh god!" My voice is muffled, breathless, as I explode around his fingers. I can feel a slight tremble in my limbs as he releases his deliberate hold on my throat,  his hand trailing lower to support me,  caressing my breast through the corset top.

"Mmm. That's my good girl. Coming apart for me so beautifully." A soft kiss below my ear as the fingers of his other hand continue to move in me, working me through the last of my explosive orgasm. "Now, you're ready."

He removes his hand, and I turn my head to look at him, the sudden emptiness an unexpected ache; but he reaches down, our fingers intertwining as he leads me further into the dimly lit corridor.

# Chapter Seven

## *Quincy*

**R**ather than taking me into one of the many rooms we passed with the wide windows designed to cater to those who enjoy exhibitionism or with voyeuristic tendencies, he leads me to the end of the hall, around a corner and down another set of stairs. This floor, like the one above, is set in darker tones, but the rooms are private, with no signs of windows for passersby to view. There are much fewer doors here too than the floor above, but he passes by all of them, not stopping until we reach the very last one.

I hear a soft beep, and glance down, startled to see a thumb pad, similar to the one used to get into the club. He opens the door, and waits, brow quirked.

I glance hesitantly at the thumb pad once more, before looking back at the masked adonis standing before me.

"It's just an extra security measure. It doesn't lock the room, just registers which member is borrowing it, essentially. This floor is for private suites, and can only be accessed by members who pay for the more. . . detailed. . . service."

Ah. Right. I almost forgot for a moment that I was in an exclusive sex club, where only the wealthiest and most notable names can gain entry.

Which means, this guy in front of me is probably just another rich, self-entitled asshole like most of the other men upstairs.

*What the fuck am I even doing here, again?*

*Oh, right. Dammit. I'm doing this for the bucket list. Get fucked, for Eli. I'm doing this for Eli. God dammit, Eli!*

**With a shaky breath, I enter.**

Calgary
Cougars

# Chapter Eight

## Bash

**I** stand to the side, waiting, curious to see if she will take that next step with me. I can see the uncertainty on her face, even after I had her totally blissed out only minutes before. She doesn't know just how good it can be between us yet. She doesn't understand how I already own her body. Her pleasure, her orgasms are for me alone. I know she feels this connection that flows between us like electricity but unlike me, she may not yet understand what it means.

That's alright. She will. I'll make sure of it.

Glancing pensively from the scanner by the door, back up to my face, there is something in her expression that I can't quite place. But in a blink, with well-practiced intention it's gone, smoothed away into a more neutral calm. But I saw it. Similar to the look I had seen upstairs, but now that I am up close and personal? There was no hiding that particular emotion from me.

That look again. It was fear, not just apprehension over experiencing something new, someone new. Who put that fear in your heart, beautiful girl? That icy fury is back, simmering under the blazing heat of desire. I know that look. You will never have to be afraid of me. And I'll make sure you know it if it's the last thing I do.

With a shaky breath, she steps forward into the dark space. She crosses the threshold, the motion activated lights switching on, illuminating the room in a soft glow.

Unlike upstairs, the rooms on this floor are cast in a more subtle opulence. The deep maroon of the walls offset by rich mahogany furnishings, accenting the dark satin sheets. Following closely, the door closes behind me, locking into place with a soft click. She jumps, spinning to face me, eyes wide behind her lace mask; I raise my hands slowly, a soft grin on my face.

"No tricks here, Sunshine. You're safe with me." There is still a hint of uncertainty in her gaze. Well now, we can't have that. I step to the side. "The door locks automatically from the inside when in use, so no one outside can enter without permission. But you are not trapped, you can leave at any time." I gesture for her to try the handle. "Go ahead, check for yourself."

Her gaze flicks to me once more as she steps forward, testing the handle. I can hear the sigh of relief when the knob turns and she is able to crack the door open slightly, only to close it once more.

"This is only going to work if you trust me. I don't want there to be any doubt in your head. I'm not going to push you to do anything that makes you uncomfortable, okay? And if at any time you want to stop, just say the word." I shove my hands in my pockets, rocking back on my heels as she faces me once more. "I can see you have some hesitation, and I'm assuming this isn't something you have done before?"

My attention is drawn to her lush lips as she bites down on it nervously, before shaking her head.

"I need your words, honey. You have to talk to me or this isn't going to work."

"I – I'm. . . No, I'm not new to exploring, but I haven't been to a club like this before either."

I nod. Ok, I can work with that.

"Not new to exploring, how?"

She hesitates again, and I raise an eyebrow, silently challenging her.

"I had a partner. I was her . . . she was my . . ."

Silently, I wait.

"For a short time, I had a partner that was my dom."

My eyebrows shoot up in surprise. Ok, well damn. I wouldn't have pegged this dark vixen as a submissive, but you never can tell a book by its cover, I guess. I'm not unfamiliar with the dynamic of dom/sub pairings, but given the fact that I have not pursued any sort of genuine relationship in years, it is not something I have personally explored much outside of the occasional role-play. As her confession truly registers, surprise gives way to an underlying annoyance. It is completely irrational; I know how irrational it is, but just hearing the words come out of her mouth that she was submissive to another partner grates on my nerves, like a splinter just under the skin that I can't quite remove.

"And do you typically lean towards dom/sub partnerships?"

Shaking her head, she bites her lips as she glances down at the floor, taking a breath before looking up at me once more. Relief washes over me like a cool bath. No extensive history of play then. No, that will be for us to explore together.

"No. It was something new that I had been trying. Something I felt I needed at the time, but to be honest, I wasn't really a good sub."

"Oh?" My curiosity is piqued.

"I don't like giving up control." She shrugs, nonchalant.

"And yet, you found yourself coming to a sex club which caters heavily to BDSM play?" This woman is full of surprises. I carefully refrain from making a witty response about the whole 'brat' dynamic that can come into play in a dom/sub relationship, she is skittish enough without me pushing her on the matter. There will be time for that later.

"What can I say? There were some things about the BDSM lifestyle that I still find. . . entrancing." Her gaze is bold now, a fire blazing in her eyes as she meets my gaze head-on.

I can't help the grin that breaks across my face. Oh this is going to be so much fun.

"Before we start, I have a few rules." I step closer, closing the distance between us. "First, and most important, you need to pick a safe word. Something completely out of context from our activities here in this room. Having been in a dom/sub relationship before, I assume this concept is familiar to you?"

She nods, pupils dilating as I step into her space. Unable to stop myself, I reach out, running a knuckle gently down her soft cheek before tucking a loose strand of hair behind her ear and eliciting a soft shiver in response.

"What is your safe word?"

Her eyes close momentarily, but when she opens them again, there is not a hint of fear or hesitation in her eyes. Only desire.

"RBG."

My brow furrows, head cocked slightly. "RBG?"

She nods firmly. "Yep."

"Why RBG? What does it stand for?"

Shaking her head, her lips purse in contemplation, but I can see the mirth in her eyes as she responds.

"Does it really matter?"

I bite my tongue, curiosity warring with my impatience to feel her again. "No, I guess not. Not right now, anyway."

This beautiful woman grins at my reluctant acquiescence, dimples showing, and I have to catch my breath as it distracts me from my curiosity. She can tell it's going to bug me, but she isn't going to elaborate. And I find myself no longer caring. Not at this moment. I don't know what it is about her. There is this magnetic force that draws me in and I can't stop myself from leaning in to kiss the corner of her mouth where it meets her dimple.

Surprised by my own lack of self-control, I force myself to take a step back, giving us both some much needed distance. I swallow.

"Good. Second rule. No names."

My new addiction tilts her own head now, mirroring my earlier action.

"May I ask why?"

I hesitate, unsure of how to answer. Normally, I have no problem with women knowing who I am. Most of the events I go to at this club do not include masks, and my face is well-known here in Calgary, being one of the home team's star defensemen. Honestly, it's hard to go anywhere in this city without being recognized, with hockey being such a big sport in this area.

Do I sometimes use my name and stardom to hook up with women? Sure. I don't know a single hockey player who hasn't from time to time, especially with the puck bunnies that follow us around on the circuit; and I'm certainly not ashamed of my hookups. But this isn't just another random hookup. This night, this woman, feels different; electric. All-consuming. It's awakened in me desires that I haven't felt in years. A need I no longer recognize in myself.

Already, I feel a level of desire, a need to own her, to possess every part of her that is completely out of character for me. I never let myself get attached, not anymore. And yet, I have a feeling that if I let it, this could easily turn into more than a moment I wouldn't want to forget. And that, right there, is dangerous territory. So for both of us, for now, until I can get a better handle on my own intense emotions, it's better if this remains anonymous. Because if I were to know who she really is, there would be nothing stopping me from giving in to my dark desires and truly making her mine.

"You don't have to answer that."

Apparently my hesitation was a little too obvious.

"It's fine. I don't need to know your name, you don't need to know mine. I'm not from the area, anyway. It's better this way. I'll just call you. . ." She taps a finger against her chin, pondering. " . .Biscuit."

A stone sinks in my gut at her words. Not from the area. What does that even mean? Clearly she's here. And then the second half of what she said registers and my head rears back in mock disgust.

"Biscuit? As in the food?" It couldn't be a hockey reference. There's no way she can recognize me with this mask on, and as we already established - no names, so it's not like she could know I'm a pro athlete.

She grins once more, those irresistible dimples begging to be kissed. "Yep. Biscuit. That shall be your call-sign."

"No, no no. I need something more masculine than that. Sir, or mister, or fuck-god-extraordinaire, adonis. Anything along those lines. But no food nicknames." I wrinkle my nose. "It's too cutesy."

A roll of her eyes is the only response I get.

"I can see why you feel that you didn't make a good submissive. You definitely have a bratty streak. How about we just don't call each other by any names? Keep it simple? Ok, good. Moving on. Third rule."

"Jesus. How many rules do you have?" She scoffs in mock annoyance.

"Just one more. And then we can go over your limits." I cut her off before she can respond. "Now listen close, because this is really important." I pause for emphasis, making sure I have her full attention. "Alright. Now. The most important thing to remember is not falling in love with me. It will be heaven, I will rock your world, but you cannot fall in love with me. I don't do relationships. Keeping our names out of this will help keep a necessary level of detachment, I think." I nod to myself. "Yep. That should do it. Now, let's go over your limits."

"Hey now! Wait up one god damn minute!" Her voice is outraged. "What the hell? Don't fall in love with you, are you serious?"

My face is grave as I nod. "Very." She has no idea how deadly serious I am.

# Chapter Nine

## *Quincy*

"**W**hat the hell? Don't fall in love with you, are you serious?"

"Very."

'Don't fall in love with me.' Is he for real, right now? Seriously? I give him a skeptical once over. I mean, damn, he's freaking gorgeous. And yes, the level of attraction I felt from the moment our eyes locked upstairs is completely unexpected, but he could use a bit of a reality check. Tonight is my one night of freedom. A night to let loose and be totally uninhibited. After tomorrow, I go back to real life and all that entails. No more Cinderella in her ballgown . . . er, corset and heels. It is motherhood, messy buns and running a small business. I don't have time to fall in love with anyone, least of all a gorgeous and intense stranger that I met after midnight at a sex club in a strange city. There will be no shining prince on a white horse to rescue me from my reality.

"You do realize, this is a random hook-up in a sex club, right? The whole 'no strings attached' rule is kinda implied here. But sure, whatever. I promise I won't fall head-over-heels for you as long as you don't fall madly in love with me. No obsessed stalker shit, got it? That stuff's fun and all when it's in my romance novels, but I could do with less of it in the real world."

His brows furrow quizzically but I don't bother elaborating.

Swallowing down my discomfort, I force a confidence I don't feel as I continue. "As for my hard limits, like I said, I'm open to exploring." I shrug, nonchalantly. "I do have one rule though. My corset stays on. You can play with my breasts, pleasure my pussy all you want, but the corset stays on. You move to take it off and I will safe-word. Got it?"

His frown deepens, a look of confusion marring his gorgeous face, but I don't elaborate. He can make up all the ridiculous rules he wants about no names, one night only, and no falling in love with him, blah blah blah. But he has to give me this. It took months before I felt comfortable in my own skin with Mistress Simone. Not that she would have accepted anything less from me once I fully embraced the nature of our partnership at the time.

Rather than responding to my one and only demand, he steps closer, taking me in from head to toe with a slow once-over that makes my body flush from the intensity of his gaze. I tense as he moves within a hairsbreath of me, my eyes closing involuntarily as he trails the back of his knuckles down the side of my face and I let myself just feel him. His presence is all-consuming and it's hard to think with him standing so close to me, touching me.

"You sure there's nothing else?"

Hesitating only a moment, I bite my lip nervously as I shake my head, my body blazing with awareness, the room feeling overheated as his fingers skim lightly down my neck, grazing the top of my breasts. I inhale sharply as he leans close, his lips brushing against my ear as he commands softly, "On your knees."

I pause, biting my tongue at the cutting reply I would normally make. My hesitation is brief, but he still catches it and I see the sardonic raise of his brow as he waits silently. Submit or leave. Now's the moment, if I'm really going to go through with this. Taking a steadying breath, instead, I find myself lowering slowly to the pillow on the ground, eyes downcast.

"Good girl."

I can feel his watchful eyes as he circles me deliberately, his words almost nonchalant. A soft tickle brushes across my skin where he trails a feather across it, and I can feel a path of goosebumps raise everywhere he caresses me with that gentle touch. A shiver I can't suppress escapes me and I hear the rumble of his low chuckle.

"Are you nervous?"

A slight nod is all I can manage.

"What's your safe word?"

His voice is nothing more than a whisper as it tickles my ear, his soft fingertips blazing a trail down my back and lighting a fire in my core.

"R-RBG." I clear my throat, staring at his feet as he moves to stand in front of me.

"Good girl." Reaching out, his hand caresses my face as he grips my chin, tilting my head up so that I am forced to meet his gaze, his eyes dark and full of a hunger that can't be ignored. "Then let the game begin."

# Chapter Ten

## Quincy

A thrill of anticipation courses through my veins as he circles around, fingers trailing across my jaw with the lightest caress as he moves. Stepping behind me, I feel his legs frame either side of mine from where I remain kneeling on the floor. A shiver travels down my spine, goosebumps raising the hair on the back of my neck as he leans down, his lips brushing my ear.

"Do you want to play, Sunshine?"

I bite my lip, nodding, as nervous energy wars with the tingling awareness passing over me; his nearness igniting a burning need that warms me from the inside out. A sharp sting has me gasping as he nips at my ear.

"Your words, Sunny. Show me you can use your words like a good girl."

Licking my lips, my voice cracks, and I clear my throat, trying again. "I – I want to play. . . with you."

"Mmmm." He moans softly in my ear. "That's much better." Kissing away the sting from where he nipped, I tilt my head, wanting to lean into the sensation of his lips on me. But just as quickly, he is gone, pulling back my long hair away from where it hangs down my back. My eyes close as I feel him slowly wrap the strands around his fist, and his mouth is on me once more, trailing sensual kisses in a path down the side of my neck and across my bare shoulder.

A firm tug on my fisted hair has me tilting my head back, pointing up towards the ceiling, and my eyes open to stare up at the textured pattern lining the dark ceiling. And then he kisses me. Our mouths connect for the first time, and my world explodes into a chaotic blend of sensation as my eyes close in surrender. The taste of his lips, the feel of his tongue gliding along my seam, his teeth playfully nipping at me, urging me to open for him. And I do so willingly, greedily accepting everything he offers. His tongue meets mine, sensual and teasing and I could just melt into a puddle.

I've never experienced anything quite like his kiss. Not with Elijah, or Simone. Not with anyone. His mouth is commanding, his presence all-consuming, his grip on my hair tightening to the point where I can just barely register pricks of pain through the drug-like ecstasy of the moment I am quickly becoming lost in. Moaning, I feel like I'm falling as I lean further back, giving myself over to the moment and honestly, if I fell to the floor I probably wouldn't even care. Instead, he catches me, bracing me against a solid wall of muscle.

Breaking the kiss, I blink up, dazed, and find him licking his lower lip, his eyes hooded, mask blocking most of his features. But that look as he gazes down at me? It's more than desire, more than need. I can feel it connecting us on a tangible level, tying us together in this moment. Gently guiding my head upright, he releases me and steps away. It's hard not to whimper at the sudden loss of his warmth but his words distract me.

"Eyes forward, hands behind your back."

I don't think twice as I move to do as he says, and I hear the rustle of fabric before something soft is binding my wrists together.

"No taking off the corset, you said?" He comes to stand in front of me, his thighs touching my front and he's so tall that I have crane my neck to look up at him.

"No taking it off." I confirm, my voice low and husky, lips still tingling and swollen.

"Hmm. That's a real shame." He tilts his head, gazing down at me. "It's a crime for something so . . . enticing to stay in such . . . pretty wrapping." He reaches out, trailing his fingers across my chest as he speaks, eliciting another chill of delight. "That's alright. We can find other ways to play."

He takes one step back. Then another. And I wait anxiously as he takes me in, like an appraiser looking at a new piece of art in their collection, carefully observing me. I can only imagine what he must see, the angle of my arms tied behind my back causing my breasts to be on full curvy display through the tight corset as I continue to kneel before him.

Cocking a brow inquiringly, his gaze heats as he glances down at my chest once more. "Your breasts, beautiful? Are they off limits?"

"N-no?" My voice is breathy, my tone questioning. I'm not sure how he intends to play with them without taking off my restricting top but I am open to whatever he wants to try.

Moving forward once more, one hand trails along the top of my chest, then the other, in opposite directions before calloused fingers slide between my breasts and the corset. The friction of his large hands create a spine-tingling barrier between my soft breasts and the snug-fitting top. His fingers trail further inside, finding my nipples and gently teasing them, the next thing I know, my breasts are popping out, looking ridiculously large in my peripheral vision as they are pushed up by the boning of the corset.

"Much better," he purrs.

He continues to play with me, running soft circles around my areolas before flicking and pinching. My nipples are hard, aching for so much more than his calloused fingers and I whimper.

"You like that, beautiful?"

"Yes."

I wish I could see his face. For the first time since entering the club tonight, I am resentful of the masks that were part of the required dress code. The anonymity provided by the masquerade theme provided me relief upstairs, being so out of my element in this strange environment. But now I find myself wishing desperately to see more of his face, to see his full expression as he takes me in, rather than these glimpses offered by the partially-blocked view the covering offers.

"Your mask. . . please. . ." I bite my lip, fighting back another moan at the shock of his mouth as he drops to his knees, sucking one nipple into his mouth. My breasts are heavy, aching with need, and he takes the other into his large hand, kneading and massaging the overly-sensitive flesh.

Pushing my chest out further, I lean into his wet heat as his tongue circles me, sucking and flicking before turning his attention to the other side. The silky material holding my wrists firmly in place chafe against the delicate skin as I futilely tug against the restraint, needing desperately to run my hands over his body, through his hair, rip off the mask. Anything.

His mouth pulls away with a pop, and I bite back a groan at the sudden loss of wet heat. He tsks, shaking his head at me.

"Patience, Sunshine. Be a good girl for me."

"But I -"

He pinches one nipple, the bite of his fingers, eliciting a sharp gasp at the sting. He releases me quickly though, soothing the hurt with his mouth, tongue licking over my nipple in a sensual caress.

# Chapter Eleven

## Bash

I am painfully hard, cock throbbing in time with my racing heart as I take in the sight of my dark vixen. She is absolutely breathtaking, this quivering mess now kneeling in front of me. After playing with her generous breasts, I can't help but tease her further with a few more languid kisses, before motioning for her to stand just long enough for me to guide her over to the bed. Wordlessly, I make quick work of removing her short skirt. The sight of her in her corset top and crotchless panties, thigh highs, and heels have my cock leaking with a desperate need to possess every inch of her.

Instead, through clenched teeth, I take my time; forcing myself to maintain the same patience I just admonished her for needing. With slow deliberation, I kneel before her, one hand reaching out to hold on to her curvy waist, keeping her balanced. Lifting one leg, I trail my hand from thigh to calf, tracing over the delicate material of her thigh high stockings, lingering on her inner thigh and the back of her knee before making my way down to her red heeled boots.

I waste no time sliding my hand over top, unclasping the velvet bow and removing the shoe before lowering her foot gently to the ground and proceeding to follow through the same motions on the other side. With her hands still securely tied behind her back, I know she can't reach out to hold on for support, and I won't risk having her fall by having her try to step out of them herself. And as much as I want to fuck her in her heels, my need to taste her in this moment is all-consuming. So getting heels off and into the bed is the priority right now. Guiding her backward the few remaining steps until the back of her legs connect with the edge of the bed. I make quick work of lifting her and she gasps.

"Oh no. I'm too heavy! You don't have to - oof."

Unceremoniously, I drop her on top of the mattress, cutting off the remainder of her ridiculous protest. The fact that this stunning woman could think for one second that she was too heavy for me has my blood thrumming with the need to throttle whomever made her think that way in the first place.

"I'm going to stop you right there, Sunshine." As she sits before me, I slowly work at the buttons of my black dress shirt, making a show of taking off the material, carefully making sure she sees every inch of muscle as the shirt falls to the floor. Her eyes devour every inch of me, and I have never been more thankful for the countless hours I spend in the gym each week.

My voice, gravelly with need, dark desire lacing my words as I continue, "You are a fucking goddess. Every damn inch of your curves were made for me. And if you think for one damn second that I can't handle you, then I'm going to need you to move up to the headboard, grab the headboard with both hands and sit that fine ass on my face. Right. Fucking. Now. Now, turn around gorgeous."

Her mouth drops open in shock at my filthy words, and after a brief moment to process what I said, she awkwardly fumbles to shift fully onto the bed. Turning her back to me to follow my instructions, I stop her briefly, making quick work of the knot in my tie which I used to bind her wrists together.

"Now hold on to the headboard, honey." I slap her ass, eliciting a small squeal as she crawls to the top of the large bed.

I unbutton my slacks, providing some much needed room for my throbbing dick but choose to leave them on as I crawl up the bed behind her. Once she has firmly grabbed hold of the headboard, I wrap my arms around her middle, pressing my front to her back and leaning in to kiss her ear.

"Mmm. Such a good girl, following my instructions."

A smile tugs at my lips as she leans into my kiss, and I slap her pussy with a loud smack, eliciting a shocked gasp.

"And that's what happens to good girls when they are naughty and talk badly about something that belongs to me.We treat my possessions like the -"

"I didn't - ah!"

I smack her pussy again.

"Don't lie to me, pretty girl. You implied this fucking spectacular body was too big for me to handle."

Nipping her ear, she moans, and I smack her pussy again, before running a firm hand along her slit. God, she is soaked. Absolutely drenched for me.

"But this body doesn't belong to you, it's mine. And I take care of what's mine."

One last time, I smack her pussy, this time hard enough to make her cry out from the shock of the sting. Before she has a chance to react, however, I am pulling away from her back, quickly sliding onto the bed between her legs and my mouth connects, swiping along her dripping cunt.

"Oh!"

Startled, she lifts up, pulling away from me. That simply won't do. Turning my head, I gently nip at her inner thigh, growling, "I told you to fucking sit on my face." Grabbing her hips, I firmly pull her down, holding the full weight of her against me as my tongue swipes out, connecting with her pussy once more.

"Oh! Oh, fuck!"

She moans, legs shaking around me as I take my time, thoroughly enjoying my meal. She tastes divine, like salt and sweet sunshine. Fucking ambrosia on my tongue. I swipe through her folds like a man starved, inserting my thumb to play with her clit while my finger reaches for that sweet spot. Her whole body starts to quiver, muscles tightening around me in response, and I moan against her, showing her just how fucking delicious she is.

"Oh, oh - I don't want to hurt you. Jesus, this feels so fucking good! Oh, god!"

Trying futilely with shaky limbs, she lifts up a fraction, but I reach up with my other arm, cinching it around her thighs and pulling her firmly back down to my greedy mouth.

Turning my head slightly, I rub my scruff against her smooth inner thigh, knocking my mask askew, but I am too far gone to care.

"There's no 'god' in this room with you, honey. Just me." Running my tongue upwards along her thigh, I insert two more fingers, pumping in and out. "And when my tongue is eating your cunt, it's me you'll cry out for.."

I've lost my damn mind. She doesn't even know who I am, but at this moment, I can't think straight past her delicious cunt and addicting moans of pleasure. Cinching my arm more firmly around her thighs once more, I pull her down so firmly that she loses her shaky grip on the headboard and nip at her pussy lips before soothing the sting away with my tongue. She gasps, and I pull her clit into my mouth, sucking hard.

"Oh fuuuckk! I'm gonna - I'm - I, oh!"

She explodes around me, soaking my face with her cum, and I lap it up, not wanting to miss a fucking drop as she slowly comes down from the high of her second orgasm of the night.

Through the restricted amount of movement offered by her tight corset, she leans forward against the headboard, trying to catch her breath. I use the opportunity to slide out from underneath her, licking my lips clean before running an arm across my mouth as I take her in. She's a beautiful fucking mess, hair wild—the tie that had been keeping it out of her face long since fallen out—and skin flushed, breathless and quivering all over. I quickly fix my mask before leaning over to kiss her on the corner of her mouth.

"Such a good fucking girl. You are so goddamn gorgeous when you come for me, Sunshine."

I pull myself away from her, climbing off the bed to grab a condom from one of the decorative baskets atop the nightstand, and push my pants down.

Head resting on her arm, she tiredly turns her face to look in my direction and I smirk as she takes in the sight of me. I move forward towards the edge of the bed, taking my aching dick in hand and giving it a hard stroke, making a show of it for her.

"Oh shit! You're huge!"

I know I'm not the biggest dick around, but I'm well above average, obviously larger than she is used to seeing, and I can't hide my amusement at her shock, despite the underlying irritation that settles on my chest at the thought of her doing this with anyone other than me.

"I promise I'm just the right size for you. Now come here, gorgeous."

She slowly makes her way over to me, a goddamn wet dream with her breasts on full display, still held up by her corset. I watch with hunger as they bounce around as she makes her way over to me. I could spend the rest of my life buried in her tits and I would die a happy man. Slowly pumping myself, my arm flexes with restraint as I give her a show in return. She makes me feel like a goddamn teenager, my cock leaking for her, pulsing with desire, and it takes every ounce of willpower that I can muster up just to keep my shit together. My jaw clenches, muscles straining with the urge to let go of my tightly wound leash I am keeping myself tethered to. She stops in front of me, tentatively reaching out to run her soft fingers over my toned abs and I can't help the shiver as electricity shoots through me.

"Can I -" She bites her lip, nervously glancing down at my swollen dick before back up at me, her gaze hooded through her own lace-covered mask.

Swallowing thickly, I can't speak, so I nod instead.

"Um -"

My brows furrow as I watch her glance from where she kneels on the bed, to me standing before her. After a moment, realization hits. With her corset on, she can't easily bend over to reach me, and she is determined not to take the damn thing off.

"Lay on your back, Sunshine. Head hanging over the edge of the bed."

Without hesitation, she moves into position, and before I can fully prepare myself, she is reaching out to grab me, arching up to lick a bead of pre-cum of my tip as she takes me in her small fist.

"Jesus! Fuck!" I hiss. The smallest of touches has me fighting for control and I am about two seconds away from coming all over her beautiful face and tits.

"Oh sorry! Did I – did I hurt you?" Immediately, she goes to release me, but I reach out, wrapping my hand around hers and holding it to the base of my cock.

"Put that fucking mouth back on my dick, right now, Sunshine. Goddamn, you feel incredible."

A shy smile crosses over her face, her features working to unravel me. This girl definitely has a pleasure kink, and that is something I can absolutely work with.

Instead of going for the tip, this time she reaches out, tongue tentatively licking along the base of my piercings. I moan in response, my hand tightening over hers, encouraging her to pump me as she continues to work her tongue over my Jacobs ladder. She continues to lick me, driving me wild as she circles around each piercing before taking me into her mouth, and stars explode in my vision.

Holy. Fucking. Shit.

I'm not deep, only about halfway in as she starts to suck, her fist pumping me with more confidence. Pulling out slightly, I give her a chance to catch her breath before I am shoving back in, deeper. Again, and again until we find our rhythm, until I am fucking her mouth and she is gagging, tears leaking out the corners of her eyes and trailing past to fall inside her mask.

Fuck! I need to see her. Need to be inside her. To own every damn inch of her perfect body. My heart is racing, my chest about to explode. I can feel the corners of my vision going dark as my balls begin to tighten. Fuck. No. I can't come yet. I need more. I rip myself out of her mouth with an audible pop, leaning over to quickly grab the condom that lay forgotten on the bed next to her. I glide it over my dick which is so hard it could cut steel and climb onto the bed with her. Grabbing her by the ankles, I yank her down so her head is fully resting on the bed once more.

"I can't wait any longer, honey. I need to be inside you. Right. Fucking. Now."

Her legs are slick with need, her cunt glistening as I move over her, spreading her wider as I settle between her legs. Taking a breath, I try to calm myself down. I need to go slow for her, need to pace myself. She is relaxed and ready for me but it's still going to be uncomfortable for her. I push forward until the head of my cock is inside.

"Shiiiiit. You are so goddamn tight." The words come out in a hiss. My breaths are labored, arms shaking on either side of her head. "I need you to relax for me, Sunny."

Reaching down with one hand, I play with her clit as I slide further inside her wet heat. She feels fucking incredible. Absolute fucking heaven.

"Oh! Oh my- oh my god!"

Leaning down, I take her nipple in my mouth, sucking and laving it with my tongue as I continue to play with her clit and push deeper and deeper until I finally bottom out. In unison, we groan, our vibrations adding to the delicious friction.

"I'm gonna fill you up. You feel so fucking incredible. Goddamn, you are going to ruin me."

I kiss a line up her neck, sucking and biting before landing on her mouth. She opens for me, our tongues colliding in a tangled frenzy, and I can't help it. My hands glide up, touching and teasing before caressing her jaw. I tilt her head, deepening our kiss and my hand continues up, tangling in her silky hair. Goddamn this fucking annoying – my fingers tangle in the silk tie of her mask, and with a huff of annoyance, I slide the damn thing off, without breaking our kiss.

Our bodies are connected, moving in time to a sultry dance that only we can hear. Breathy moans and hums of pleasure fill my ears as I barely register the filthy sounds of our bodies coming together. I'm gonna fucking explode, I am so fucking gone for this girl but I need to see her. Need to see her come just one more time.
With one last kiss, I pull back, sitting up and shifting the angle and she cries out in pleasure.

"Right there! Oh – oh right there! Yes, don't stop. Please, please don't stop."

"Fuck, gorgeous. I'm gonna fucking come. Gonna fill you up so damn full that I will be leaking out of you for days."

My vision is blurring, everything is a haze of need and she fucking comes. With the sexiest cry I have ever heard she comes hard, milking my cock and I look down to watch the awe on her face and something pulls at the back of my mind, fighting against the intense pleasure coursing through me.

It takes me a minute, my brain working at a snail's pace as it wades through the heavy fog of bliss clouding my thoughts. She looks so damn familiar. Have I fucked her before? Oh Jesus, fucking shit. This feels so damn good. No, I would remember this. Remember her. There's no way –. And then it hits me like a freight train.

Holy. Fucking. Shit.

Is that? No – I can't believe –

I explode, a million stars blacking out my vision as my balls tighten and erupt and I swear I have what has to be a fucking out of body experience. Hell, I think I may have even blacked out for a minute.

Lying together, limbs tangled, chests heaving, desperate for air, I turn my head, running my hand through the familiar long dark strands of hair. Brushing them out of my dark vixen's face, I tuck the strands gently behind her ear and stare into the totally blissed out face of -

Holy shit. It's fucking her! Holy mother of -

# Chapter Twelve

## Bash

'**N**o obsessed stalker shit, got it? That stuff's fun and all when it's in my romance novels, but I could do with less of it in the real world.'

Her words echo, playing on a loop through my head as I step out onto the dark street. The words went straight to the backburner when I was thinking with my dick, but once reality slammed back into me and I realized the woman I had my dick inside was fucking Quincy. . . well, given what I know, it all came rushing back to me with crystal-fucking-clarity and slammed into me like a goddamn freight train. In the moment, it was easy to dismiss the words but now I know them for what they are.

And now that I've had her? Knowing how she feels? What she tastes like? How our worlds collide in what could be nothing less than cosmic fucking intervention? I told myself that if I had her for the night, if I made her mine, it would get this strange fucking obsession out of my head and be able to move on with my life? Now? Well, there's no going back.

The chill from the early morning air has a bite to it, and I pull my collar up higher, hunching my shoulders, leaning into the jacket's warmth as I try to block out the icy breeze. Careful to avoid the piles of partially melted snow that sit in grime-filled patches along the side of the street, I make sure to give myself plenty of distance as I follow behind my new addiction out of the discreet building. Where the hell does she think she's going, dressed like that? It's four am. If she thinks for one goddamn minute that I'm gonna let her walk around by herself in a strange city –

I'm fully prepared to follow her on foot if necessary, but I am pulled from my darkly spiraling thoughts as she comes to a halt halfway down the street. Stopping at the edge of the Valet drop, I'm careful to keep out of her view, and watch as she pulls out her phone. Relief floods me momentarily as I realize she must be arranging for a ride, only to be immediately replaced by anxious frustration. What the hell is she doing calling for a ride? She doesn't seriously think it's a good idea to get in the back of a stranger's car?

Easily recognizing me without the mask, it takes mere moments for the valet to bring me my Vantage S while I stand here, and I reluctantly pull my gaze away to thank the man. He didn't even wait for me to present him with the ticket stub before he had the sleek Aston Martin idling in front of me. I may not be a regular at this club, but I am well-known in this city. The guy is eager to please, but thankfully, remains professional enough that doesn't try to engage me in conversation about tonight's game.

Not bothering to even look, I hand him a generous tip and slide behind the wheel, training my gaze once more on the temptress still waiting down the street. Unease fills me as I watch her fight the chill in the air, shivering in her too-thin jacket. Clearly she was unprepared for our blustery winter weather. Maybe I should get out and offer her my jacket? Maybe I should offer her a ride instead? I could say I just happened to see her while I was leaving, but then she may recognize my face.

Impatiently, I sit, waiting,. . . watching. I'm sure the valet attendant must wonder what the hell is wrong with me, that I haven't left yet but I don't give a damn. I'm not leaving until my girl does. A car pulls up next to her, a sign in the window indicating that it works for one of the more common ride-share companies, and she leans down to speak with the driver. Seconds later, she slides in the back seat. No thought or care given to the fact that she is a woman alone in a new city, getting into the back of a stranger's car, just trusting that they will take her to her destination safely.

I'm tempted to storm over there, to show her just how dangerous trusting strangers can be. Instead, I clutch the wheel until my knuckles are white, fighting back the urge to chase her down and drag her into my own car. The ride-share pulls away from the curb, and carefully, I follow.

No obsessed stalker shit.  Ha. Well this would definitely fall within that category, I can't help but think of the irony as I drive down the quiet city street. The sky is slowly shifting into lighter shades of gray as the sun prepares to rise with the impending day. When I came to the club, desperate to seek an hour or two of reprieve from the memories that haunt me, I had no idea that I would come face to face with my destiny. Let alone that I would find myself in the same position as one of my closest friends, literally stalking a woman who wants nothing to do with me, when I could literally have my pick of almost anyone else I want. I have been giving my best friend crap for years over doing the same damn thing and I am just as unapologetic in my need to keep her safe, just as Theo had been with Danni.

And let's be honest, how could it be anything less than kismet? The mystery woman that I felt an all-consuming need for just happens to be the same woman connected to my closest inner circle, one with whom we are so closely interconnected she is practically an adopted part of my chosen family? Hell, if it weren't for my chaotic game schedule there were many opportunities where we most likely would have met over the years. It's ironic that our meeting just happened to be tonight, in my city, in my playground, a whole country away from our shared friend group and her normal life. . . just days before I was supposed to finally meet her. I thought I would be able to fight the temptation, this obsession but fate had other plans. No, she doesn't know it yet but Quincy is mine.

The car pulls up in front of the Jubilee Inn, a modest hotel in a chain that's local to the area. I pull up behind them, careful to leave enough room that she doesn't bother looking in my direction and park under the covered car port meant to be an unloading zone. Still, as I watch her step out of the car and rush through the revolving door. My relief from seeing her safely back to her hotel is short-lived as I unbuckle and I quickly follow behind her.

It's not the worst place to stay, though it does show signs of aging, the lobby dimly-lit and paint on the walls a faded yellow that I am sure was once meant to be bright and welcoming.If I had my way, she would be put up in a five-star resort. Somewhere with better amenities and security. Somewhere where someone like me couldn't easily follow in pursuit without being noticed. That's something we'll have to fix in the future.

For now, I content myself with watching her cross through the lobby and step into the elevator, making sure to stay out of her direct line of view. The doors close and I move closer, my longer stride quickly making up the distance between us. Within seconds I'm pressing the button to signal the next car, making sure to watch the numbers light up above hers. Slowly, the numbers light up, indicating each floor before finally landing on the number eight. Lucky number eight. I can't help but tap my hand against the side of my thigh as I wait. Come on, come on. Hurry up already. I'm gonna miss her.

A soft chime signals my elevator's arrival and I quickly step in, pressing the number eight and breathing a sigh of relief as the doors close before me. The short ride up is the longest few seconds of my life and finally, after what feels like an eternity, I arrive on her level. It seems fate is once again on my side, because the doors open and I am just able to catch her as she steps into a room about halfway down the hall. I wait a beat, holding my breath in anticipation as I listen for the soft click of her door being shut in the otherwise empty hall before stepping out and following.

Four doors down, then three. . . two more and then. . . room eight o' eight. The stars keep aligning in our favor, a shimmering golden strand connecting the dots of our inevitability, even if she doesn't know it yet. I can't help but grin at the overwhelming satisfaction and sense of rightness of it all. I've got you, Sunshine.

# Chapter Thirteen

Bash

"**A**hem"

Nothing. Seriously?

"Excuse me. I'm so sorry to bother you."

The bored attendant finally looks up from where she had been staring at her phone on the counter. Turning on the charm, I give her my full mega-watt smile that has melted off the panties of countless puck bunnies.

"I'm so sorry to interrupt, but I was hoping you might be able to help me."

I pause, waiting for some sort of response. Blinking several times, she just stares up at me, as if in shock. I wait a moment. Either she is a hockey fan that knows who I am and is completely shocked by the fact that I am standing in front of her now, or she just can't register that someone is at the front desk this early in the morning. Still no response. Alrighty then.

"You see, I've gotten myself kind of into a mess, and I was really hoping you might be able to help."Well, my girlfriend is upstairs. You see, she's in town visiting. And I thought I would run out to grab us both some breakfast. You know, surprise her when she wakes up?" Holding up the pastry bag and cup-holder sitting with two steaming cups of coffee to add credibility to my story, I continue. "But I . . . well, I feel like such an idiot, but I left my room key on the nightstand. And I would really hate to wake her up and ruin the surprise. I was hoping you might be able to help me out and give me a new key?" Pasting on a sheepish expression, I give her my best puppy-dog eyes for good measure.

Unresponsive, the young woman continues to stare up at me and I pause, beginning to wonder if this was a terrible idea. Of course it's a terrible idea, you idiot. You're a well-known public figure and if you're caught lying and trying to get into a random woman's hotel room you will absolutely meet the brutality of cancel culture on social media, if not also facing possible jail time and risking your career. She rapidly blinks again, jaw slack, and then -

"Ohmygod! You're him! It's you!" She points to the jersey I quickly changed into when I ran home to change after concocting this asinine plan while loitering in the hall eight floors up.

"If by 'you', you're referring to "Tricky" Adamare from the Calgary Cougars, then yep. It's me." Playing into the sheepish 'well, shucks, you got me' vibe, I shrug, pasting on a look of rueful amusement.

"Oh my god! I can't believe it's really you! You're here! Oh wow! My dad's never gonna believe this!"

She went from slack-jawed to starry-eyed in seconds. Yep, definitely a hockey fan. It's not surprising, around these parts. And honestly, I'm hoping I can use it to my advantage. Leaning my elbow onto the grimy counter, I try not to grimace at the visible layer of grime that covers the old check-in desk, setting the tray with the 'breakfast surprise' down next to me.

"What do ya say? Think you can help a guy out?"

"Of course! Let me just pull you up in our system!"

"You see, that's the thing. The reservation is under my girlfriend's name. Usually she stays with me when she's in town, but she wanted this to be a surprise visit, which is why she's at a hotel to begin with. But I can give you our room number?" I give her that charm again, hoping to allay any concerns that she may have.

"Oh. I didn't realize you had a girlfriend. The news always mentions that you're single. . . "

"Yeah, we have been trying to keep our relationship pretty quiet. She doesn't like all the attention from the media, and I can't say I blame her. It can be a lot to handle."

Her cheerful exuberance dims slightly at my response, but she bounces back quickly. "That's not a problem. Let me just call up to the room to verify-"

"She's probably still asleep though. I – well. . . I kept her up really late last night. I was just so excited to see her at the game, especially with our big win and all. I would hate to wake her up for this, she probably needs the rest. I was just hoping to drop off the breakfast for when she wakes up before I have to head out to my practice. Got an early morning today before we fly out to Vancouver for our next game. You know how it is." I shrug, nonchalant, as if this girl would know what the life of a professional athlete with a rigorous travel schedule actually entails.

"Here, if it makes you feel any better, I can show you my ID. I don't mind signing any paperwork too, if it's needed for the replacement key?" I throw another cheerful grin in her direction, containing my amusement as she flushes. "And you would be really helping me out, you know. I would be so grateful. . ." My words trail off, a note of longing in my voice.

"Well. . ." The girl glances at her computer before looking past me at the still-empty lobby. Biting her lip, she continues. "What was the name on the reservation?"

"It's under Quincy Crawford. We're in room Eight o' Eight."

The 'we' really seems to seal the deal for her. Or maybe it's the fact that when she pulls up the reservation, she can confirm that there is, in fact, someone by that name staying in that room. There is still a bit of hesitancy as she glances back up at me, and I can see it warring with her need to not disappoint someone who she recognizes as being a local celebrity.

"We're not really supposed to do things like this -"

I would sure as fuck hope not. But in this instance, if I can get her to bend the rules for me, I can shove down my anxiety and frustration over the fact that my girl is staying in a hotel with such lax security protocols. If it works in my favor, their employee's slip-up will save me the hassle of having to reach out to Finn. I know he absolutely could take care of the situation for me, but I'm not ready to explain myself to him quite yet. In time. All in good time.

"I completely understand. You are just doing your job and I wouldn't expect anything less from such a wonderful. . ." I quickly glance down at her name tag, continuing "hospitality coordinator. Either way, I really appreciate your help, Rebecca."

Shyly, she glances down at the countertop, and this time the blush goes from the roots of her hair, down to her neck.

"I guess I could make an exception, just this once." She looks up again, her eyes bright with wonder at me saying her name. Generally speaking, I have always hated when celebrities and athletes use their status to bend or break rules, but when it comes to the beautiful vixen on the eighth floor? My honor flew right out the window along with my reluctant control the moment I realized who she was.

After signing several pieces of paper, and offering to take my picture with the girl, I was finally able to walk away with a spare key to match the room number I had chased down earlier this morning. Making my way over to the elevator, I carefully raise the hand holding the tray of coffees and grin in her direction and she waves back as the elevator doors close before me. For good measure, knowing there's a chance she could still be watching, I press the button for the 8th floor.

I do not, however, stop there. The chime signals the landing and as the doors open, I quickly press the button to close them once more. I'm sure my beautiful Sunshine is still sleeping in after her . . . workout last night, but I don't want to risk the chance of running into her if she's not. Instead, I head up to the 10th floor, depositing the breakfast tray in the closest trash and making my way down the hall to the staircase at the far end.  All I needed was the key, for now. From here, I can sit and wait in the car for her to leave, before making my way back up to her room.

I'm gonna have a real, honest-to-god stakeout. Haven't had one of those in ages. At least, not since Danni was dealing with that fucker Brad. And am I gonna get fined for missing my final practice before the short holiday break? Sure. But it will absolutely be worth every damn penny. I know where my girl lives. . . well, relatively speaking that is. It's information I'll have to obtain from either Danni or my brother, but I'll cross that bridge when I get to it; but I know the general area that she lives in. I also know exactly when and how we are supposed to meet.

But that doesn't happen until we are back in Washington, and I can't wait that fucking long to see my girl again. Not when she mentioned to me last night that she was going to be attending a concert today. Not when there is every real possibility that something could happen to her. Or she could meet another guy to hook up with.

My heart races at the thought, the irrational urge to punch someone making my fists clench. It's not an unreasonable assumption. I did meet her at a sex club and she did technically hook up with a complete stranger, after all. Besides, she's alone in a strange city for god's sake. I'm offended that our little friend group didn't reach out to me and arrange to hang out with her to begin with. . . For her protection, of course. . . Well, no matter. I'm about to fix all of that.

# Chapter Fourteen

## Quincy

Goldie: You alive over there?

Sissy: Forget that! Did you fuck anybody?

Finn: Uh. . . why am I a part of this chat?

Jay: I second what he said. Why are we here?

Goldie: In case she ends up dead or kidnapped. Duh!

Goldie: You two are our techie muscles to find out if anything bad happened using your magic computer sleuthing skills.

Finn: OR . . .

Finn: You could just wait and see what she says

Jay: By this point, she can pretty much take care of herself.

Finn: We really didn't need to be included in this

Goldie: EXCUSE ME! She hasn't responded yet.

Goldie: For all you know, she could be lying dead in a ditch somewhere

Goldie: Oh my god

Goldie: I sound like Ma

Sierra: The way I cackled at that *Laughing emoji* *Laughing emoji* *Laughing emoji*

Finn: *Eyeroll emoji*

Jay: Or she could still be enjoying herself *Suggestively raises eyebrow emoji*

Jay: Oh god. I'm sinking to their level

Goldie: One of us! One of us! One of us! Hehehe *devil emoji*

Sissy: The next day???? It couldn't have been that good!

Sissy: Wait! Was it that good?

Sissy: Details, woman! Give us details!

Oh my god you guys are ridiculous. You are blowing up my phone.

I was trying to sleep.

Sissy: Ma'am! That's NOT an answer. Just tell us if it was good.

Me: . . .

Goldie: Like. . .?

Yes it was good.

Sissy: Man? Woman? Multiple? Details lady! Give us details!

Goldie: Toys! Were there toys involved?

Goldie: In terms of chili peppers, how spicy was it?

*Finn has left the chat*

*Jay has left the chat*

He was good. Ok? Like REALLY good. Jesus. Now go get a life you two. I need to get some sleep.

**E**ver since I gave birth to Wolfie, I have been an extremely light sleeper. Becoming a single mother will do that to a person. Truthfully, I had been forced to learn to sleep with a sense of wakefulness for years before that anyway. At least since my mom had married Sierra's dad. Fight or flight is no joke, and the body does what it needs to protect itself. Maybe that is why I was so surprised to find that when I woke today, it was with the early winter sunlight of midday shining through the gap in my dingy hotel room curtains. Jesus, I slept like the dead.

I stretch lazily, like a cat basking in the sun, as I feel every delicious ache of my thoroughly worked muscles. Flashes of last night, of my mystery man and all the dirty things he said, the feel of his hand and his mouth and huge cock filling me, flash through my mind and I can't help the wide grin that spreads across my face. Last night was wild. Something so completely out of character for me. A truly once-in-a-lifetime experience. Now, I have to look forward to a wonderful evening reconnecting with Simone and her wife at the concert. Another bittersweet moment to cross off my bucket list before I have to head back to reality. But for now, I think, I'm gonna be really self-indulgent and stay in bed just a little. . . bit. . . longer.

"Hi baby! How's my favorite little wolf today?"

I force a cheerfulness into my words that I don't feel. I miss him so damn much that it's almost painful. Technically, I have only been gone a little over twenty-four hours at this point, but trying to talk with him on the phone just isn't the same. He's had sleepovers with Danni in the past. It's something we started while I was taking night classes to finish school, and even after I'd graduated, we still continued the weekly overnight visits to maintain his routine, at least we had until Danni's stalker situation had escalated to a point where it was unsafe to continue. But that's over now, and we're trying to get Wolfie back into his normal routine.

Still, I've never been this far away from him, and it makes me uneasy. I know it's irrational, the underlying fear that clings to me like a dark shadow. On a logical level, I know Ray is behind bars. He can't get to me, can't hurt Wolfie. . . but even after all these years, it still gets to me at times, the worry and what-ifs.

"We're doing great over here! Aren't we, Wolfie?" Danni's voice is cheerful as her face comes into view on the screen, interrupting my spiraling thoughts. "We had a good breakfast, and looked at our airplanes. And after lunch, we're gonna go check out that awesome new gym that Uncle Theo put in for us, huh, bud?"

I smile, listening to Danni recount their morning for me. Danni is so great with him, she always has been the best unofficial aunt and godmother. I'm so thankful to have her, especially with Sierra living so far away.

"That sounds great. I know you guys are going to have so much fun. Mommy has to go take a shower and start getting ready for tonight. I miss you so much, my Little Wolf. I will be home soon, okay? Just one more sleep, and then Mommy gets to go on an airplane, just like your airplanes, to come home to you. I love you so much. Be good for Auntie. " I see him on the screen, and though he doesn't acknowledge my words, I know he is listening.

"We've got this, QT. You have fun and cross that item off your bucket list, okay?"

I don't want to hang up, but I know I really should shower and get ready for the day. I'm supposed to be meeting up with Simone and her wife, Layonna for lunch and a shopping trip before we hit up the concert tonight. Danni can see my hesitance though, and I appreciate the fact that she still tries to reassure me. "Go!" she continues, laughingly. "I promise we will call if anything comes up, but we're fine here. Uncle Theo and I have this handled. Plus, Finn is planning to come visit his favorite little guy tonight and have dinner with us. Everything will be fine."

# Chapter Fifteen

## Bash

**I**t has been hours of sitting here in my car, strategically parked at an angle where I have a good view of the hotel entrance. Despite the waiting, it's been a productive morning. After dealing with a very pissed off coach for missing my morning practice, I spent another two hours on the phone calling in favors and making plans. The longer I sat here thinking about the connections between Quincy and me, the more I realized that I can't let her go. My brother and friends have done their part in helping to take care of her and her little boy over the last several years, but it's time for them to pass on the mantle.

Hopefully Sunshine was able to get some rest after how hard I worked her last night. I know from what she said, she's got a concert to get to tonight and friends to meet with before that, but she doesn't know half of what's coming her way. . .

It's half-past-noon and I perk up as I finally catch a glimpse of my dark vixen. She's dressed more modestly for the day, in black yoga pants and that damn coat again that is not fit for the frigid winter air, with her hair pulled up in a messy bun. She looks fucking stunning, and I have to fight the urge not to get out of the car and chase her down to make her come with me right now. *It's all a part of the plan, remember. You knew she was meeting up with a girlfriend. This is your one fucking opportunity to get in without being noticed. Stop being a fucking idiot and focus.* She gets into the back of another damn ride-share and it's all I can do to stop myself, fists clenching the steering wheel until my knuckles are white with my barely contained restraint.

Giving it to the count of five, I don my favorite ball cap and make my way over to the hotel. Thankfully, with the key card now in my possession, I'm able to use a side entrance meant only for guests without the risk of running into the woman at the front desk again. Rather than the elevators, I head to the stairs, taking them two at a time until I reach the eighth floor. My hand shakes slightly, though whether it's with nerves or anticipation, I'm not entirely sure as I reach for her door. It's not like I make a habit of stalking women and breaking into their hotel rooms or anything. This is entirely new to me and I know it's crossing a line, not to mention breaking several laws; but my mind flashes back to Sarah, to all the ways I failed her, and my resolve strengthens. Yeah, this is the right play.

The light flashes green as I swipe the card through the slot. With the slight click of the lock releasing, I make my way inside, closing the door as quietly as I can behind me. I don't bother turning on the light, instead, using the soft stream of daylight shining through the crack in the curtains to take in the dingy room. It really is underwhelming, and my girl deserves so much fucking better. You can tell it's a budget hotel, the worn patterned bedding looking as though it hasn't been updated since the nineties. Aside from the lone full-size bed, there's only one nightstand with an older lamp and dresser with a small television resting on top. Just your average hotel room.

Glancing around, I don't see any signs of bags or anything that may belong to her. I make my way over to the dresser, checking the drawers, but they are all empty.  There's nothing under the bed or in the nightstand either. Shit. What if she took her stuff with her? That would certainly throw a wrench in my carefully laid-out plans. I'm about to give up and head back to the car to regroup when a thought occurs to me, and I head towards the attached bathroom

With a breath of relief, I find my answer. Aside from toothbrush and toothpaste, the makeup on the counter is minimal. The only other bag is a small backpack that hangs from a hook on the back of the door. It would seem my girl travels light. That's alright. There's still a chance I may find what I'm looking for.

Carefully, I search through the big pocket, finding her outfit from last night along with what looks to be a large men's tshirt. The fuck? Where the hell did she get this? A strange sensation roils in my gut and it takes me a moment before I come to the realization that it's jealousy; an emotion I haven't allowed myself to feel in years. Angrily, I grab the shirt, fisting it into a ball and shoving it inside my jacket pocket. No fucking way. If she's gonna wear anyone's shirt it will be fucking mine. Moving on, I search the rest of the bag and finally find what I'm searching for in a small pocket off the side. Oh, honey. We're gonna have to work on your self-awareness.

Without a second thought, I pull out the small passport, flipping it open and snapping several photos before shooting them off to my guy.  The desire to pocket the damn book and take it with me too is overwhelming, but I fight the urge, reluctantly returning everything to its proper place. Soon.

# Chapter Sixteen

## Quincy

**"O**h my gosh, you guys. Thank you so much for coming with me. I'm fucking shaking right now."

It's not a lie. My hands are definitely shaky as I take another long hit off my pen. Holding it in, I feel the burn saturate my lungs and slowly release, the calming buzz finally starting to take effect. I've been with Simone and Layonna for most of the afternoon. It was great getting to see them in their new home, to see all the changes that Layonna has brought about in Simone's life. Holding hands as they sit across from me on the loveseat, Layonna shoots a small smile at Simone that warms me from the inside out. I'm so happy for them. Simone was there for me when I needed her the most, but I was not in the right headspace to give her what she needed in return. Watching the two of them together, now? It's fucking beautiful.

"You good?" Layonna looks at me with an amused half-smile and I can feel the grin stretching across my face in response.

"Yep, so good. I just love love, ya know? And you two are so freaking good together. It makes my heart happy."

I can feel my head start to nod in time to the soft buzzing in my head. It's like a melody, so chill and inviting. God, I haven't been this relaxed in I don't even know how long. Between my long days with Wolfie, and even longer nights dealing with all the business shit, it's so nice to just be. . . chill for once, with my friends.

"I think that edible is finally hitting."

Simone's voice sounds further away, but that can't be right. She and Layonna were right here, weren't they? I peek through squinty eyes. Did I close them?

"Oh yeah. I did that."

Wait, was that in my head?

Alright, maybe I am a little buzzed. But damn, it feels nice.

"Come here, sweetie."

"How strong did you make those brownies?" Simone's voice peaks through the pleasant haze, chiding tone reminding me of the times when I was decidedly not being a very good girl. I giggle. I definitely was not a good girl last night either. I think my mystery man even called me his naughty minx once.

"You can wear some of my clothes tonight."

Am I floating? I glance down to see that Layonna has grabbed my arm as she leads me up the stairs. Oh, right. We were supposed to be getting ready for the concert. Instead, we got carried away, catching up and just having a good time. Layonna gave me one of her new brownies to try. More than one? Yeah, I definitely had two. . . I think. Maybe I should have stuck with one, but it just feels so fucking good. Oh well.

I'm in a daze as they lead me to their bedroom where Simone turns me and directs me to sit on her bed. Laying back, I cackle as the room spins around me.

"What are you laughing at?

Simone has always been too serious. I'm glad she has Layonna now to lighten her up a bit. Turning my head, I sniff and catch a whiff of something fruity and flora.

"Mmm. You both smell so good. He smelled good too. Not like you. But still good."

I turn on my side, trying to get more comfortable, and see Simone and Layonna give each other a funny look.

"Who smelled good, sweetie?"

"Hmm? Oh." It takes me a minute to process what they are saying. "He did. My mystery man. He smelled like leather and spice and was soooo. . ." My voice trails off, and I'm distracted by thoughts of him and all the delicious things we did together last night. He was delicious. "yummy."

"Alright, pet." A soft hand runs through my hair, making me smile. The touch is soothing. It reminds me of him. "Why don't you rest for a little while? We have some time before we have to get ready for the concert?"

My eyes feel so heavy, and I breathe in the comfortingly familiar scent of the cozy bed as I close my eyes. A set of soft lips brushes against my head, followed by another. Voices follow soft footsteps out of the room, but I can't make out what they say.

It's okay. I'll just rest here for a minute. . . .

"Holy shit. How strong were those brownies?"

I'm not sure how much time passed before I was woken by two overly cheerful voices, and I squint in annoyance as I look around the darkened room at them.

"Oh, now. They weren't that strong." Layonna laughs lightly, her hand waving away the thought dismissively.

"Well, babe. They were probably stronger than she's used to. She doesn't do edibles very often because of her son, remember?" Always the voice of reason, Simone cuts in before I have a chance to respond.

With a reluctant sigh, I force myself to sit up. "Your bed really is super comfy, you know."

Layonna grins, shooting a wink over at Simone. "Oh, we know. But we don't mind sharing with you. Anytime."

"You're always welcome here, pet." Simone responds.

We haven't been together in over two years, but she still calls me by my pet name whenever it is just the three of us. I guess that's the benefit of having shared something special with both of these incredible women, and anyway, old habits die hard. Slowly stretching, I take stock of how I am doing. I am still pleasantly buzzed, but definitely have more of my wits about me. That's good at least. Alright, I can work with this.

"You ready to go party?" Layonna asks with her lighthearted cheerfulness.

"Are you ready to cross another big item off your list?" Simone's voice is more stoic. She knows what going to this concert means to me; what it meant to Elijah before he passed away.

Letting out a shaky breath, I nod in response.

"Good. Then let's get you all dolled up, Cinderella."

"I'll be right back, I need another drink!" Yelling over the crowd to where Layonna and Simone are still dancing, they nod at me, grinning widely as their hips move together in time to the music.

The vibrations of the music pulse through me, the high from the remnants of the edible I took earlier along with the hits off my pen creating a fantastic zen, as I dance my way through the crowd while trying to push closer to the bar. We are in the middle of the last opening act before the headliner comes onto the stage, and after dancing for the last hour and a half I am desperate for a drink. My body is still sore from last night and just the thought of what I did brings a flush to my already overheated skin. I still can't believe it happened. It was like a scene straight out of a movie, complete with the hot and mysterious stranger.

I hate to admit it, but Dr. Sandsworth was right. Checking another item off the bucket list without Eli was hard, but the memories from last night, along with the ones I am making at the concert tonight with my dear friends, are ones that I will be able to lean on during the bad days. And I can't lie to myself anymore about the fact that this bucket list looming over my head has been holding me back, preventing me from fully letting go and moving forward with my life. I forgot how nice it can feel to just. . . live.

The crowd is so into the music that they don't even notice as I pass by, dancing my way through the pulsing crowd, to the beat of Glitterpuss's newest hit. Glow sticks and black lights bounce off the neon colored clothes of scantily clad men and women who are dancing like there will be no tomorrow, and I let my body relax, swaying to the beat as I continue to push through the crowd.

Finally breaking free from the standing-room only floor space, the crush of people lessens and I take a deep breath of the slightly-less stale air. I can still feel the vibrations coursing through me as I make my way through the back of the large club over to the bar. There is a line of people waiting for the bartenders to take their orders, so as I slide into the back of the line, I let my eyes drift closed and continue to sway to the heady beat.

Lost to the music, I'm not sure how long I have been standing in line. It could have been seconds, or minutes, but I don't care as I relax into the music.

That is, until I feel a hand slide up my skirt from behind and grab my ass.

My startled yelp is lost to the music, and I doubt anyone around me even noticed as I jumped in surprise.

With quick reflexes, I turn to face Mr. Handsy, forcing his grabby paw away in the process.

"What the hell?"

He meets my glare with an almost oily smile.

"Hey, baby. How about I buy that fine piece of ass of yours a drink?" I can barely hear his shout above the music. The oily smile takes on a smug look as he throws me a wink. Seriously. As if this sort of shit actually works for him.

"Are you for real?"

Unable to stop myself, I roll my eyes. "Keep your hands to yourself, jackass." He's totally killing my buzz right now, and I'm annoyed as fuck. I'm supposed to be relaxing and living in the moment dammit, not dealing with another handsy asshole.

He steps closer, sliding into my personal space like he belongs there and I glare at him, taking two steps back, arms crossed over my chest as I try to mask my growing discomfort. Maybe I should have brought Simone and Layonna with me.

"Hey, baby. No need to be like that. I just thought I would show you a good time tonight."

Again, he states this as if he is doing me a freaking favor. As if I wasn't having a good time all on my fucking own, thank you very much. And now he's ruining my buzz.

"I'm not your baby, asshole."

Not bothering to wait for a response, I turn my back to him, flipping him the bird over my shoulder as I shuffle several feet forward to follow the line that has moved up.

He tries to say something again, but I deliberately try to focus on the feel of the music, losing his voice in the chaotic flashing lights and thrumming beat vibrating through me.

Another step forward, and it's my turn to order.

But the man has grabbed my arm, pulling hard to turn me in his direction. "Come on, baby. You don't need to be such a bitch about it. I was just trying to buy you a drink."

I try to pull my arm free, but he won't let go. And fuck, his grip is so tight it actually hurts. Schooling my features, I refuse to let this drunk asshole see how much he is starting to bother me. I try my best to ignore the hand squeezing me as I turn back to place my order.

"What'll you have?"

The bartender looks bored, not even bothering to spare the asshole grabbing me a second look. As if he sees this shit every day and it doesn't phase him.

Futilely, I try to yank my arm free but the asshole won't let go. I throw a look over my shoulder, glaring at him and am startled when he is suddenly pulled off of me.

"She'll have a Roy Rogers." A new voice interjects.

What is with these men? Ugh!

"No, she will not! She is having a cran vodka. Make it a double!" I insert myself into the conversation, annoyed that these jerks are totally ruining my fun. I gave myself one night to let loose. One night where I had friends with me and I knew I would be okay to drink and have a good time, and these jerks are totally ruining it for me. It doesn't even register that the voice speaking over my head knew my order. In fact, through the buzz that is making my thoughts all fuzzy, it takes a minute to register that the voice is a familiar one.

The bartender just nods, acknowledging my order before making my drink. Since the jerk finally let go of my arm, I close my eyes, nodding along to the beat as I try to find my vibe again and become one with the music.

"You wanna tell me why the fuck you had your hands all over my woman?" The other man's voice interrupts once more, pulling me out of my happy place. As his voice registers through the fog, I find myself just as frozen as the asshole who had grabbed me. His tone is lethal, his expression frozen fury, as I turn slightly to glance up into the face of the man before me. The man from last night. I may still be buzzed, and he may have been wearing a mask last night, but his voice and profile are unmistakable, even through the haze and the very dim lighting of the noisy venue.

"N-no man. It was just a misunderstanding. Honest." The coward has his fucking hands in the air and I could swear he is shaking. Literally shaking at the sight of this menacing, bulky man towering over him. Not that I can blame him. I would be too if that cold fury was pointed in my direction.

"Double Cran Vodka" A voice calls out my order.

With my arm now free, I quickly move to grab my drink. Not wanting to deal with that shit-show behind me, I turn in the opposite direction, making my way back towards the crowded dance floor. A minute later though, I am not surprised to feel the soft pressure of a familiar touch in the middle of my back, and I allow him to guide me to the side of the crowded room.

"So we meet again." The music is so loud he has to shout for me to hear, but there is no mistaking the grin that breaks across the face of the handsome devil standing before me.

I take a long sip of my drink, chewing thoughtfully on the straw.

"Now tell me, what's a girl like you doing in a place like this?"

My nose wrinkles in disgust at his question.

"No good? See, here I am trying to give you more of that classic pick-up line you were looking for last night. How about this – hey, gorgeous, did the sun just come out, or was that just your beautiful face smiling up at me back there?"

A laugh escapes me before I can stop myself, and I shake my head as I respond.

"Do those lines seriously work for you?"

"Yeah, Sunny. They do." He throws me a wink.

"Sunny?"

"Well, like I said, that look you gave me back there? Pure sunshine. And since I don't know your name . . .yet . . ." He draws out the 'yet' waiting for me to fill in the blank, but I am not giving in that easily.

I shake my head. "Nope. You said no names, remember?"

Though I can't hear it over the music, he shakes his head with a resigned look on his face and I can see the sigh as he lets out a breath.

"Alright then, Sunny it is."

There is a shift in the beat as the song ends, transitioning into the intro as Jericho takes the stage and my eyes widen, a true smile crossing my face. "Oh my god! I love this song! I have to go find my friends!"

Not waiting for an invite, he grabs my free hand, using his large frame to shield me from the crowd as he pushes us forward. Before I know what's happening, he has shifted us around so that I am now in front of him, and holy shit, he has led me to stand directly in front of the stage. Like, right in front of the lead singer. Well beyond where I had been standing before with Simone and Layonna. We hadn't been able to reach this far, with so many people pressing forward to get as close to the stage as possible.me. But now? This view is incredible. I could practically touch the lead vocalist from this distance. I never thought I would have the chance to get this close to a performer I have idolized for years.

I turn my head to face my mystery-man, throwing a wide grin in his direction as I shout "Thank you!" back at him. He doesn't respond, and I am not sure if he even heard over the loud music and cheering crowd. Instead, as I look back up to the stage and start swaying to the beat, I feel a jolt of awareness as warm arms encircle me from behind, and I am pulled into the comforting warmth of his chest as we dance together.

The rest of the concert is spent like this, with his arms around my waist, dancing along to the beat, just soaking in the music. As the final song starts to play, I squeal in surprise as I feel myself being lifted into the air.

My shout of surprise dies off as I find myself sitting on Mystery Man's shoulders. His freaking shoulders! Holy shit!

"Put me down!"

I can hear the slight panic in my voice. I may be short, but I am all curves, and I'm well aware of the fact that I'm no delicate flower.

He doesn't listen. Instead, his hands squeeze my thighs gently as he steps even closer to the stage. Leaning forward, which puts me at an almost precarious angle, I can't help the squeal that escapes my lips.

"What are you- ?"

A hand is reaching out to me. Holy shit! Is this real life?

The singer is leaning down, and our faces are at eye-level with each other. And he is freaking holding out his hand to me!

With shaky fingers, I reach out, and his hand grabs mine.

Holy. Fucking. Shit. He's grabbing my hand. I'm sitting on some dude's shoulders that I only just met last night, towering over the rest of the crowd, and the lead singer of Jericho is freaking grabbing my hand and singing directly to me. I could die and go to heaven. How is this real life?

# Chapter Seventeen

## Quincy

"There you are! You disappeared on us. Did you have fun?" Layonna calls, drawing my attention to where they are standing as I exit the venue.

"Oh my gosh, you guys! I found him!" Running up to my friends, I throw an arm over each of their shoulders, hugging them both. Simone pulls back from Layonna, reluctantly breaking apart from their quiet moment from where they stood waiting for me.

"Found who, pet?" She inquires, as Layonna looks on with a bemused expression.

"My mystery guy! He's here! It turns out he likes the same type of music and we just happened to run into each other at the bar. How crazy is that?" I grin excitedly. Okay. I may still be the tiniest bit drunk. And buzzed. But I am so happy right now. So light I feel like I'm floating. When was the last time I felt this free? Unable to help myself, I step back, twirling as I take in the stars tonight. They are so beautiful.

"That's your mystery man?" Layonna cuts through the haze, her voice questioning. Oh yeah, he was supposed to come with me. Turning slightly, I look for the mystery guy in question, checking to make sure he is still with me. I can feel him as he steps closer behind me, his presence sending tingles of awareness coursing through my veins once more.

"Hi, I'm -"

Jerking around, I slap a hand over his mouth. "Uh uh. No names!" I chide, interrupting him with a scowl as he tries to introduce himself to my friends. I've been having one of the absolute best nights of my life - last night not-withstanding - and I know it largely has to do with my mystery man here. No need to go and complicate things by adding names to the mix. "We made a deal, remember!" I'll be damned if he goes and ruins it now when I am so clearly on a winning streak.

He nips at my hand covering his mouth and grins over at me as I jerk away with a squeal. "Alright. No names." He chuckles and I damn near swoon. It's still dark, but lighter outside than it was in the venue. Seeing his face, without the mask, the chiseled jaw and dimples peeking through his scruff, he looks so familiar. Why does he look so familiar? I squint up at him, tilting my head to the side, as if that would help me think more clearly through the fuzzies floating around in my brain.

Brows furrowing, he looks at me with an amused expression on his face. "You good?"

Must be because of all the things we did last night. I swear I've never met him before. I would not have forgotten if I had seen that face in real life. And there's no way I would ever forget that voice, all dark and rumbly. Yeah, it must just be from last night. Or maybe he just has one of those faces. You know, the kind of face where people go 'Wow! You look so familiar, I feel like I know you, but in fact, you do not know them. Yep. I bet that's it. Nodding to myself in satisfaction, I take his hand in my own before turning to face my friends once more, only to find them both gaping at me in stunned silence.

"You -"

"You're -"

They say in unison, mouths agape.

Ha. That's a funny word. Agape. A – gape. Snickering, I repeat the word in my head.

"Hi. Yep. I'm me. And you lovely ladies must be friends with Sunny, here." He smiles broadly, sticking out his hand as he introduces himself. Kind of.

Those damn dimples again. Even peeking out through the scruff, I can see them just enough to be practically melting into a puddle over here.

Collecting themselves, Simone and Layonna each take turns shaking his hand, and that reminds me, I should be introducing everyone.

"Oh shoot! Yes, sorry. These are my friends, Simone and her wife, Layonna. This is my mystery man from last night. You know. The one I told you about?" I waggle my eyebrows exaggeratedly. And boy did I tell them? In great detail, over brunch with mimosas. If it were anyone else, I probably wouldn't have said as much, but Simone knows me in a way different from my other friends. There's a certain level of trust that was built upon our former intimacy, and with our shared history, I trust her judgement to give me a sense of clarity that I don't always have myself.

"You were talking about me, Sunny?" His tone is smug and I look over to see the pleased look on his face. "All the dirty little details?" He lowers his voice, and the sensual tone has my core throbbing for him once more.

Thinking back to our earlier conversation, recounting all the details that were discussed from last night. . . and those that I didn't share. . . I can't help the blush as memories flood through me.

"Yeah, well" I shrug, trying to appear less affected than how I feel. "What can I say, it was a novelty experience. Plus, you did help me with that creepy old guy, so. . ." Yeah. There is that. After tonight with Mr. Handsy, that makes it twice in a row where my mystery man has come to my rescue. Maybe after all of these years, my luck has finally turned a corner. Closed the door on the harsh reality of my past, as it were. Huh. Now wouldn't that be nice. Too bad nothing in life is ever that simple.

"Oh, so I'm just a convenient bouncer, is that it?"

"Eh. Maybe something to that effect." I try for uncaring but I don't know if I totally pull it off.

"Uh huh." He drags out the words, eyeing me slowly up and down. "Well then, shall I continue to play your personal bodyguard and escort you back to your hotel for the evening?" His eyes are full of promise that heats my blood.

"Um, are you sure. . ."

"Now pet," Simone and Layonna both interject. "You were going to come back to our place tonight, remember." Her words are firm, leaving no room to question. That hadn't been the plan. They were gonna take a ride share with me and drop me off at my hotel on their way home, but I know they're just trying to be protective.

"Guys, it's okay. Really." My gaze flicks from my friends, up to my mystery man. "I would like to spend more time getting to know my new . . . friend, before I have to go home tomorrow."

"Qui-"

I shoot a glare at Layonna, cutting her off before she gives me away. Sighing, she comes to my side, leaning in to whisper in my ear.

"Sweetie, do you know who this is?"

I glance from Layonna to my mystery man on my other side.

"Uh, yeah. I already told you, he's the guy from last night."

"No, but like, do you know who he is?" She hisses in my ear. Layonna is usually the more laid back of the two women, and I frown at her now. "He's -"

"Stop. Do you somehow know who he is?" I throw back at her.

Layonna's mouth snaps shut, lips flattening as she glances at said man and then back at me. "Yes, and you should too. He's -"

"Is he a criminal?" I cut in.

"Uh, gonna speak up for myself here. No criminal record on file." Mystery man interjects, sheepishly waving at my friend.

"No, he's not a criminal, he's -"

"Is he dangerous?"

"Not that I know of." Layonna's voice is reluctant before Simone eyes me, interrupting with a murmured, "Maybe to your pussy, dear."

My cheeks feel like they are on fire, cutting through the haze from the alcohol in my system, but at this point I'm not sure if it's because of my mystery man watching on in amusement to our conversation or the piercing way that Simone is looking at me. She always could see right through me.

"Uh, gonna interrupt here again. Not that you would take the word of a stranger, but vouching for myself, I'm not a danger to Sunny here. I can promise you that. I won't let anything bad happen to her."

His voice is so serious that I glance up at him but he isn't looking at me, his full attention is now on Simone.

Her gaze narrows, considering him.

"You're sure you want to go with him, pet?"

I bite my lip, nodding, before I catch myself. Words. I remind myself. Simone has always been big on clear verbal consent. Swallowing down my nerves, I respond. "I'm sure. . ." Glancing up at my surprise companion for the evening, my gaze lingers on him even though I speak to my friends. " . . . I don't know why, but I trust him. I'll be okay. I would like to spend a little more time with my new friend before I have to leave tomorrow."

"Fine." Layonna's voice cuts in with a huff.

"But if you try anything, mister. . . "

His laugh breaks through, startling all of us.

"Do you have your phone with you?

"Yes. . . why?" She responds, eyeing him with suspicion.

 "Turn on the camera to record."

Ok, now I'm not sure where he is going with this, either, but Layonna listens, and shows us all that the camera is, in fact, recording a video before pointing it back towards my mystery man as directed.

"Alright, I'm sure you all know who I am, but this here is my girl Sunny. We met at a club last night and had a grand old time together and happened to run into each other again tonight. I would like to spend time getting to know my new lady friend a little better so, if she is amenable, I would like to take her out for another round of drinks before escorting her safely back to her hotel. I promise that I have no ill intent towards her and will do everything in my power to keep her safe. If anything should go wrong, you can and should submit this to every media outlet with my full permission. Is that good enough?"

Okay. Well, I certainly wasn't expecting that. And I don't think my friends were either. Layonna just shakes her head in disbelief but stops recording. Well, I guess that's that then.

# Chapter Eighteen

## Quincy

"**O**kay then. . . What's your favorite color?"

I scowl. Favorite color, really?

"Come on, Sunshine. You have to have a favorite color. Everyone does. For instance, mine was blue." His smirk catches my attention, eyes drawn to the deep dimples in his chiseled face.

"Was blue?"

"Yeah, it was. But yellow is quickly becoming my new favorite color."

"Oh?" I arch an eyebrow.

"You know. Yellow? Like your sunny disposition."

His face is smug as he teases me, and I throw a fry at his face, muttering under my breath. "Smartass."

With lightning-quick reflexes, he shifts forward slightly, catching the fry in his mouth. Grinning widely,  he clenches it with his teeth as he shows off, before eating the damn thing whole. My eyes focus on his enticing lips, watching the way his jaw works, Adam's apple bobbing as he swallows and I shift uncomfortably in my booth as my mind is drawn back to images from last night as they replay on a loop in my mind.

"Or you know," he continues, a thoughtful expression crossing his features, voice lowering to a seductive timbre "maybe my new favorite color is black, like the color of the outfit you wore last night."

His gaze is heated as he slowly takes me in, and I know his thoughts can't be too far from my own. I can feel the sting of my burning cheeks. He slides a drink in my direction, and anxiously I reach out to take it from him, taking a large gulp to try to calm down my racing heart. Swallowing, I nervously tuck a strand of hair behind my ear as I blurt out, "Pink. My favorite color is pink."

Eyebrows raised, a smirk pulls at the corner of his mouth once more and for the first time, I am feeling self-conscious for all the wrong reasons.

"What? What is that look for?"

"I knew you were a sunshine and rainbows kind of woman underneath it all."

Brow furrowing at his words, I shake my head in confusion. "Underneath what, exactly?"

"Oh, you know. That whole "gorgeous curves, wicked grin, but 'come near me and see what happens attitude'?"

"Really? I wasn't aware I was giving off any vibes. Not that it seemed to bother you too much when you just happened to rescue me from unwanted attention last night. Or at the concert, for that matter."

His shrug is nonchalant, but his expression is somber as he responds. "What can I say? I have always been a sucker for a damsel in distress. Landry shouldn't be allowed within ten feet of another woman on the best of days. And when he's been partying?" His eyes harden, mouth flattening into a tight line. "Let's just say, he's one that it's best to avoid like the plague. God knows he's probably had enough STDs over the years to be considered a profligate."

"So let me get this straight, you saw this moderately decent-looking, albeit plus-sized, woman from across the way giving off prickly cactus vibes, and would have walked on by, but then 'Lecherous Landry' came at her and you said 'Nope. Hard Stop. Gonna go save that prickly chick from the dude with the grabby hands and leering gaze'?" I roll my eyes at the high-handedness of it all.

"Um, no. I saw an incredibly gorgeous woman with 'fuck-me' curves and intelligent eyes looking bored out of her mind, and would have come to say hello anyway, but was still working up the nerves to do so when I saw a man who honestly wouldn't have even been allowed into a place like that if it weren't for his family name and money encroaching on your personal space. And while I assumed you could handle it, I decided to jump in to lend a hand in case the asshole didn't want to take 'no' for an answer."

My laugh comes out unfiltered, loud and barking, and my eyes widen in horror at the harsh sound as his smirk spreads into a full-blown panty-melting smile. "What's so funny, Sunny?"

"Um, 'fuck-me' curves and intelligent eyes? You can't honestly say that I'm your normal type. You look like the kind of guy who would normally date supermodels, not women like . . . well, like me." I make a sweeping gesture from the top of my head, hair limp and makeup that I'm sure has smeared after countless hours of dancing at the concert down to my voluptuous figure.

A scowl crosses his face as he responds, "I'll have you know, you are exactly my type."

"Oh?" I quirk a sardonic brow at his defensive tone.

"We have fucking chemistry, Sunny. Ain't no denying it. You and me? We're good together." I laugh once more as he wags his eyebrows suggestively, shaking my head at his playful teasing, even as he reaches across the table to grab my hand, fingers intertwined.

"We were good together last night, I'll give you that." Blinking at the unexpected contact, I can't help but relax into his touch as his words wash over me.

"We are good together, Sunny. Present-tense. You and me. Me and you. We. Are. Explosive."

He's not wrong. Even now, I can feel the electrical current of awareness just from sitting across from him in the booth of this old diner. If he actually got his hands on me again, more so than just holding my hands right now. . .well, it's a good thing we agreed to just keep it to one night. The chemistry is there, stronger than it ever was with Simone, and different from the love I felt for Eli. If I let it, if I gave in to this sensation, I have no doubt that I would be swept away in the madness of this current, and honestly? I'm not sure I would care. And that is what scares me the most.

"Even if you still won't tell me your name." His voice trails off longingly, willing me to fill in the silence with the answer he has asked for no less than five times tonight.

My heart sinks into my stomach as I slowly withdraw my hand from his, and I swear that's a flash of disappointment I see in his eyes, but before I can be sure, it is replaced with another wicked grin.

"It's alright. You're not ready yet. But we'll get there. In the meantime, how about you come back to my place and we can pick up where we left off last night."

The heat in his gaze sets my whole body ablaze and I shift uncomfortably in the booth, trying to ease the ache between my legs. Trying to fight off the unquenchable desire, I reach out, taking another large sip of my drink in the hopes that it will cool this blazing desire that is building in me.

"I bet you use that line with all the ladies to get them to come home with you." My words have a bite to them that I don't intend as I attempt to deflect the need rising within me. "Besides, I thought we agreed to only one night."

His gaze travels leisurely over my body, before meeting my own, and the intensity as he looks my way knocks the breath right out of me. "I don't actually. Invite girls over to my place. You'd be the first. . . well, other than my sister, but she doesn't count. And as for our 'only one night' that we agreed to? Well, I've been known to bend a few rules when the need arises. And right now, there's nothing that I need more than to be tasting you, filling you so completely that when you go back home, I'll be the only man who can satisfy your burning desires."

Despite my best efforts, resistance was quite literally futile when it came to saying no to my mystery man. I had every intention of just going back to my hotel room and sleeping off the aching need before I had to drag my sorry ass out of bed for my flight home tomorrow. Instead, after polishing off our plates of waffles and side of fries, along with another two drinks each, I let him grab my hand, guiding me out of the booth and into the chilly late-night air.

Feeling fuzzy-headed, I blink as a blast of icy wind hits my underdressed body. With his arm draped causally over my shoulder, pulling me into his side, I'm not sure if the shiver wracking through me is being caused by the wind-chill or the man holding me against his side, but I also don't know if I care right now either way.

"Shit, you're cold."

Not waiting for a response, he quickly shifts, and seconds later, the emptiness from his arm leaving my shoulders is replaced with a seeping warmth from his jacket draped around me.

"You don't have to give me your jacket! You'll freeze!" My protests are faint at best, and he meets me with an amused glance down to see where I've already slid my arms into the oversized sleeves, belying my own words of dissent. Huh. When did I do that?

Leaning down to meet me at eye level, I blink in surprise as he instead places a chaste kiss on the tip of my frozen nose. "I'll be fine, Sunny. Let's get you home and warmed up."

At this point, I'm not even the least surprised as he pulls me into his side once more. Instead, I lean into his warmth, soaking it up like the last rays of the dying summer sun and breathing in his intoxicating scent that is a little woodsy, a little minty, and a whole lot of . . . him. Everything feels so warm and cozy, wrapped up in his jacket, his delicious scent surrounding me. I wish I could stay in this moment forever. Blinking back a sudden wave of tiredness that envelops me, I try to focus on this moment, this man holding me.

"Sure, let's go home."

Neither of us speak after that, choosing not to focus too closely on how right those words feel as he leads me down the dark street.

# Chapter Nineteen

## Bash

**"Y**ou're a fucking idiot, you know that, right?"

The room is dark, the lights from the cityscape stretching out beneath the large bay windows of my luxury apartment provide an eerie glow that casts shadows about my large living room as we enter. If I hadn't been expecting him, it almost would have been enough to make me jump, and that's saying something as I am not one who scares easily.

"Jesus, dude. Why are you sitting in the dark?"

Stepping further into the room, I flip a switch to turn on the kitchen lights, only to find Caleb along with two assholes I don't know lounging in my furniture like they own the damn place.

"My- what's going on?" Quincy's voice is soft, almost dazed-sounding as she takes in the unfamiliar surroundings.

"Come here, Sunny. I've got you." Wrapping my arm around her waist, I place a soft kiss on her temple before guiding her to the middle of the room.

"Caleb? What are you doing here?" Her voice is confused, almost petulant. This wasn't what she was expecting and I would laugh at the almost perturbed expression if the situation weren't so serious. Why does she have to look so damn cute when she's annoyed? Her nose wrinkles as she frowns, and it's hard not to get lost in the depths of her chocolate eyes as she looks from the men sitting in my living room, back to me with confusion. There's a hazy quality to her eyes though, and her face relaxes once more, eyes glossing over with a sense of detachment about the whole weird situation.

"It's alright, Quincy. You're safe." I whisper quietly so only she can hear, tucking a strand of hair behind her ear in what I hope is a comforting gesture. She relaxes into my side, and instinctively, I hug her to me, wrapping my arms around her in a snug embrace.

"Mmm. You smell good. Like leather and spice and. . ." her voice trails off, distracted as she takes another whiff of my cologne. I let out a breath of relief. I slipped up and said her name, but she's definitely too out of it to notice. Good, it's working.

"Damn, Tricky. My sister is going to kill you." Caleb lets out a long whistle as he takes in the scene.

I glare over at my friend from over her head. "Could you not?"

"Um, excuse me?" He stands, arms crossed over his chest. "Who was the one who had to fake a work emergency as an excuse to fly out here at the drop of a hat? I should be back in Washington, enjoying my lovely sister and soon-to-be brother-in-law's company but instead I'm here, in a different country, doing your sorry ass a favor. Not to mention that this is the sort of shit that would land me in a world of trouble with your brother should he ever find out. So yeah, I'm gonna give you crap for this one and enjoy every second of it."

Just as I go to respond with a sarcastic reply, Quincy's soft hum of contentment interrupts me and I glance down to see her nuzzle into my chest, eyes closed.

"Jesus, how much did you give her?"

"I gave her the exact amount *your* acquaintance told me to give her!" I hiss quietly, glaring over at my friend.

Caleb eyes her wearily, stepping closer. "And you're sure this is what you want? There's still time to change your mind. She could wake up tomorrow with a bad hangover, thinking she had a night of fun and we could leave it at that. She'd never have to know."

I jerk my head in a nod, hugging her more firmly, refusing to give her up.

"I know *exactly* what I'm doing. I'm sure." I reaffirm.

Caleb hesitates, before reaching out to place a hand on my shoulder. "This is different, man. She's not Sarah. You don't have to do this."

"Who-" Quincy tries to pull away slightly, looking up at me. I calm her with a soft kiss to her forehead, smoothing her hair back as I tuck her back into my chest before glaring over her head at my friend. Thankfully, the drugs seemed to have kicked in fully and it doesn't take much effort for Quincy to lose herself in a drowsy haze of contentment once more.

"No. She's not Sarah. She's different. Quincy is everything. And I'm not going to let her get away from me. I'm not going to let her go. I have missed out on the best damn thing to come into my life for years and right here, right now we are going to change that." I hiss quietly, trying not to disturb my beautiful captive further.

"She has a kid, man. You can't just fuck with her then leave if you change your mind down the road. She needs stability. She deserves -"

"She deserves the fucking world. They both do. You don't need to tell me that, I already know. And I'm in this. I'm all in, so stop trying to talk me out of it."

With a reluctant sigh, he steps back, nodding at his two companions for them to  join us. Standing on either side, they nod in my direction but don't say a word.

"This is Emmanuel, and Sergio." Caleb gestures to each of the men, respectively. "They work for Dante but have so graciously offered to lend their assistance to tonight's . . . needs."

Sergio pulls out his phone, grunting in confirmation before speaking to the group. "She's on her way up"

I frown, looking at Caleb, but a moment later there is a soft knock on the door. Without another word, Sergio makes his way over, letting her into the room. The woman is tall, almost as tall as me, and dressed in a sharp business suit with her hair pulled back into a tight bun. She's carrying a manilla envelope which she briskly passes to Caleb after joining our little group.

"And this," Caleb throws a grateful smile her way, "is my right-hand woman, Brianna." He addresses her directly, ignoring the rest of the group. "Did you have any trouble?"

"No. The paperwork is all in order."

He nods, a soft smile pulling at the corner of his mouth. "Good. Right, then. Emmanuel will be officiating, while Sergio and Brianna act as witnesses."

I frown as he pulls a paper out of the manilla envelope. "Wait, I thought you were going to be a witness?"

"Oh don't worry. I will be here to watch the whole train wreck in all its glory. But there is no way I am putting my name on this. No way in hell I am giving Smarty that kind of ammo to hang me with when she finds out. . . and she will find out. There's no avoiding the fact that it's going to happen."

I grimace at the thought of what Danica is going to say about all of this. She may be one of my best friends and like a little sister to me, but she has the knowledge and ability to kick my ass. And I have no doubt in my mind that when she finds out what we were doing here tonight, with one of her dearest friends and the mother of her god child, she is absolutely going to want to kill me for this.

"Alright," Caleb's voice cuts through my tangled thoughts. "Are we ready?"

# Chapter Twenty

## *Quincy*

I'm so sleepy, and this feels good. He feels good. And he smells yummy. "You smell yummy." I'm not sure if I just think it or if I say the words out loud, but his arms squeeze me a little tighter, hugging me close and I can't help but snuggle in more. Yeah. This is nice. Just like this. "Hmmm." I don't want to leave.

"Then don't." He sounds so far away. Did I say that out loud? I must have, but I don't remember. My brain feels so fuzzy. I yawn, fighting the urge to close my eyes.

"Stay with me, Sunny."

I don't know if he is telling me to stay here with him, or to stay awake. Either way, I can't. My eyes are so tired right now. I just want to sleep. Everything is warm and dark and cozy. And I am so happy. It has been such a good day. For the first time in forever, I have had a really good weekend, where I could just be me. I don't want to go back to reality tomorrow.

Wolfie.

The thought is fuzzy as it tries to push past the cotton in my brain.

That's right. I have to get back to Wolfie.

There's so much talking right now, but it feels like a bumble bee buzzing in my head.

"You still awake, Sunny?"

I lift my head, squinting up as I try to make my eyes focus. Whoa. Why is everything spinning? A giggle sounds in the distance.

"Dude, she is so gone right now. Can you get her to focus?"

Why is everyone so far away? The voices sound like they are coming through a tunnel, all echo-y and distant.

"Hey, look at me Quincy."

I turn too fast, the world spins around me and I stumble.

"I've got you." Warm hands steady me, and I giggle again.

"Look at me." A firm hand turns my face and I try hard to focus.

"Hey! I know you! Caleb? What are you doing here?" My voice is filled with wonder. Wait, did I already say that? I thought I saw him earlier but maybe I just dreamed it?

"Don't fucking touch her!" A voice growls, and I am pulled away.

What was I doing? I squint, trying to stop the spinning.

"Look at me, honey." A hand, softer this time, holds my chin. Everything still spins around me, but I know that voice. I try really hard to focus on it. Oh yeah, my mystery man. Hmm. He's so handsome.

"I need you to focus for a minute, okay honey? Focus on my voice."

His words fade away as I close my eyes, listening to the deep humming sound. That's nice. I could just listen and float into a nice. . . little. . . . nap.

"Did you hear him, Quincy?"

"Hmm?" My eyes don't want to open anymore. Why won't they just let me sleep?

"You need to repeat after me."

I lean forward until strong arms hold me again. Yep, this is nice. Right here. Nap time for me.

A soft shake jerks me awake once more.

"This is important. I need you to repeat what I just said."

I try to focus, try to listen through the cotton candy in my head. Another gentle shake, and I jerk again. Right. Stay awake.

"Say 'I do,' Quincy."

I do. I doooo. That sounds funny. What do 'I do'?

"Stay with me, Sunny. This is important. Say, 'I do' for me."

The words feel funny, my tongue feels so thick in my mouth as I try to speak. "I do." What was I doing again? Can I sleep now?

"Yeah, honey. Go to sleep, I've got you." The voice sounds far away, faded as I let go, sighing with relief as I drift into the warmth and let the darkness take me.

PLEASE TURN THE PAGE FOR A SNEAK PEEK AT THE CONTINUATION OF BASH AND QUINCY'S STORY:

# PERFECTING THE GAME
## A CORE FOUR SERIES NOVEL

Hello

Sunshine

# Perfecting the Game
## *A CORE FOUR SERIES NOVEL*

## Quincy

**"D**id you forget we're married?"

I freeze, every muscle in my body tensing as I fight the natural urge to flee. There is no escaping this though. No escaping him.

"Hello, wife."

Just in time, I turn to see him push off from the wall where he'd been leaning with arms crossed, as if waiting for this exact moment. He moves with a feline grace that belies his large, muscular form, but there is a hunger in his eyes, an almost animalistic need that his eyes hint at, as if he is the predator and I am simply the prey. And in this case, maybe I am.

"Don't call me that!" I hiss quietly, throwing a frazzled glance over my shoulder. No one can know about this. About us. "I'm not your wife!"

He raises a sardonic brow in my direction, stepping into my space and trailing his finger in a lazy, almost teasing path down my arm that sends shivers coursing through me.

"Oh? I seem to recall there being a license that states otherwise."

"That doesn't count, and you know it." Fighting the urge to lean into his intoxicating touch, I jerk away, crossing my arms belligerently.

"And why is that, dear wife?"

The bastard thinks this is funny? I could punch his stupid, beautiful face right now.

"Because you drugged me!" It's all I can do to contain the fury in my whispered shriek

## - COMING SOON -

IF YOU ENJOYED PLAYING THE GAME,
PLEASE JOIN ME ON MY INSTAGRAM
AND FACEBOOK GROUPS FOR
INFORMATION REGARDING FUTURE
PUBLICATIONS, SNEAK PEEKS AND
OTHER BONUS CONTENT

# A NOTE OF THANKS

I would like to start off by thanking each and every one of my readers. Without your support in this journey, none of this would be possible. These stories would simply remain dreams living rent-free in my mind. Every single person who has taken the time to read and/or purchase one of my books helps make this dream a reality and I thank you from the bottom of my heart for your support.

I want to take a moment to thank my alpha reader, Inge. Without your constant encouragement, this story never would have seen the light of day. After three completely scrapped attempts at getting this story right, your encouragement kept me motivated to keep writing. Thank you!

To my best friend, unofficial PA, and all-around hype-woman, Elle. Thank you for kicking me in the butt to keep writing. Every time I lost motivation, or had an ADHD squirrel moment, you helped rein me in. Thank you for being my sounding board for all my half-baked ideas and listening to hour-long voice memos almost daily while I tried to verbally untangle the messes I keep getting my characters into.

To my incredible Street Team/Beta Reader Team: Annie, Donna, Cassie, Manda, Amy, Megan, Amanda, Ashley, Kayleigh, Norma, and Maeghen, thank you so much for all your amazing work! Thank you for being an extra set of eyes and calling me out on any mistakes you find after countless rounds of edits and for your tireless work in reposting and hyping my books out in the real world. You guys absolutely rock and I couldn't do this without every single one of you.

To my fellow artists who have helped me with some incredible surprises relating to the book(s): Messterpieces and Maeghen, thank you! I cannot wait to share with everyone the fun that you have been cooking up!

I also want to take a minute to thank my family for your endless support. Thank you for showing up to my events, for encouraging your friends and co-workers to read and purchase my books and for loving me through the chaos.

Last, but absolutely not least, to my better half. Thank you so much for your support, Love. It is a lot to juggle full-time jobs and parenting and then making time in our already insane schedules to find me chances to write uninterrupted, for constantly coming up with new and innovative marketing and business ideas, for showing up for me every day with coffee and your unwavering love and support. I could not do this without you. I love you always and forever.

Thank you again everyone, for your continued support. I appreciate you! Stay safe out there!

-M.

# ABOUT THE AUTHOR

M. GEORGE IS A SELF-PUBLISHED AUTHOR WHO LIVES IN THE PACIFIC NORTHWEST WITH HER SPOUSE, THREE YOUNG CHILDREN, FUR BABY GOLDENDOODLE, AND MOST RECENTLY - GOLLUM THE BEARDED DRAGON.

SHE HAS ALWAYS BEEN PASSIONATE ABOUT READING AND WRITING. IMAGINING HER FAVORITE STORIES COME TO LIFE IN A WAY WHERE THE CHARACTERS CONTINUE TO LIVE LONG AFTER THEIR STORIES ENDED ON PAGE, AND CREATING WORLDS OF HER OWN WHERE HER CHARACTERS LIVE RENT-FREE IN HER MIND.

WHEN SHE IS NOT LOST IN A BOOK OR HER WRITING, SHE ENJOYS SPENDING HER FREE TIME WITH HER CHILDREN, SUPPORTING THEM IN THEIR EXTRACURRICULARS AND PLAYING VIDEO GAMES OR WATCHING SHOWS WITH HER SPOUSE. HER FAVORITE SHOWS LIE WITHIN THE REALM OF FANTASY AND THE PARANORMAL, AND HER FAVORITE CHARACTERS ARE OF THE MORALLY GRAY VARIETY. THE DARKER THE BETTER. . .

Learn more about M. George at https://linktr.ee/mgeorge.writesalot

Join her newsletter to receive updates, deleted scenes, teasers

and special events.

Tiktok

Goodreads

Instagram

Facebook